TIGHT ROPE

"*Tightrope* is fast, tough, and entertaining. It solidifies White's position as a newcomer to watch in the mystery field"

BEST SELLERS

"A gem of a story...damned good"

CLEVELAND PLAIN DEALER

"An engrossing mix of caper and police procedural"

BOOKLIST

The Author

Teri White won an Edgar Award fo her first novel, *Triangle*. Then came *Bleeding Hearts*, and *Tightrope* is her third–to be followed by *Max Trueblood and the Jersey Desperado*. She lives in Shaker Heights, Ohio.

TIGHT ROPE

Teri White

Mysterious Press Books (UK) are published
in association with Arrow Books Limited
62-65 Chandos Place, London WC2N 4NW

An imprint of Century Hutchinson Limited

London Melbourne Sydney Auckland
Johannesburg and agencies throughout
the world

First published in Great Britain
by Mysterious Press 1988

© Teri White 1986

Printed and bound in Great Britain by
Anchor Brendon Limited, Tiptree, Essex

ISBN 0 09 956260 X

Thanks to Ellen, Jennie, Ruth:
For help above and beyond.

Yes, I used to walk the highwire every night
Yes, I used to walk the tightrope
But it got too tight.
I walked the straight and narrow line
My head was spinning round
I worked without a safety net
But it was such a long way down.

—JUSTIN HAYWARD

TIGHT ROPE

PROLOGUE

The alley was so dark.

Tran paused at the mouth of the seemingly endless tunnel and peered into the inky blackness. He looked, knowing even as he did so that it was totally absurd, because there was no chance of seeing anything—if, God forbid, there was something to see.

His mouth was suddenly dry. He could taste only the cotton-like aridity spawned by fear.

He told himself that the fear was there simply because the alley, running between an abandoned whorehouse and a bland facade that could have belonged to almost any business, seemed so unnaturally still. It was a silent island in the midst of the noisy chaos that was swirling throughout the rest of the city. Death, violent death at least, was rarely quiet, and Saigon was dying. The streets were jammed with frenetic crowds, many of the people carrying everything they owned, all of them caught up in the same hysteria. The reason behind this wave of terrified humanity was simple: The Americans were leaving.

Tran was not surprised that they were going. He was not even startled by the undignified manner of their departure. This was no victorious march home, such as the disciples of John Wayne were accustomed to making after their wars. Not this time, not this war. Instead the brave sons of democracy were running, as panicked and afraid as everyone else

1

in the city. They seemed almost pathetically desperate to shake the mud of this stinking little lost cause from their jungle boots.

But who could blame them?

Certainly not Tran. He wanted to get away just as much as they did.

Ngo Tran was not, after all, an idiot. No one rose to the exalted rank of general, even in this army that sometimes seemed to be inspired by Gilbert and Sullivan, by being stupid. He'd known for a very long time what the end of this great Yankee adventure would be. Must be. So Tran, in his shrewdness, made careful plans.

He took a firmer grip on the small leather satchel tucked under his right arm and made one tentative move into the abyss. As he took the step, Tran wondered if perhaps his nearly paralyzing reluctance to proceed stemmed from greed rather than fear. Maybe what he wanted so desperately to flee from were not the unknown dangers of this damnable alley, but actually an all too clear understanding of what awaited him on the other side.

His partners.

Tran spit into the chasm.

He still wished that it would have been possible for him to do this alone, instead of having to bring the others into his perfect plan. But as Tran was wise enough to admit, even to himself, there was no other way. He had needed them, still needed them. What good was a fortune if he got left behind in this godforsaken place? His country was dead, yes, but there was no reason for Ngo Tran to perish as well.

The foreigners had helped him to "liberate" the priceless package he was holding so tightly and now they would do even more. His Yankee "buddies" would make it possible for him to live long enough to enjoy his share of the wealth.

In America.

Tran let a faint smile touch his lips. He liked America much more than he liked Americans. His days of advanced military training in Fort Lee, Virginia had given him a lasting appreciation of the good life available to the lucky. Big Macs. Television cops and robbers. Baseball. Soon all of that and much more would be his permanently. Even now, his wife and two children were packing for the journey.

He gave his body an angry shake. Enough of this foolishness. His partners were waiting for him and they were not patient men. Especially the lieutenant. Gathering his courage and tightening his bowels, Tran walked into the alley.

The blackness swallowed him immediately. On both sides, within an arm's reach, solid walls rose, unseen but still forbidding.

A phrase came to him suddenly, something a CIA operative once said—"Feeling like a blind rat in a dark maze." Tran had not then, or since, been entirely clear about the analogy, but at this moment the feeling was real enough.

Abruptly, without being able to see anything, without even really hearing a sound beyond that of his own tentative footsteps, Tran was aware that someone waited just ahead. He was no longer alone in the alley.

"Who?" The single word came out in a strangled whisper that was hard to recognize as his own.

There was no reply. Not one that came in words, at any rate. But there was the unmistakable sense of someone moving toward him. Tran thought fleetingly of turning to run back the way he had come. Before thought could become action, however, the unhappy realization dawned that someone was standing there, too, waiting.

Tran exhaled, making a low, keening sound deep in his throat. Who was waiting? His partners? It was easy to believe it of those tall, smiling cowboys, who spoke so easily and stank equally of cinnamon mouthwash and duplicity. Or did the threat come from someone else? Ky's people, perhaps. Had the theft been discovered too soon?

He didn't know. And, painfully, he recognized the truth that soon it wouldn't matter, not to him.

Tran dropped the leather case and the fortune that had been his for such a short time. A man more westernized might have used these last moments to reflect bitterly on the basic unfairness of life. Tran, however, fell to his knees and bowed his head. Quickly he made the sign of the cross. The least he could do now was exit this unhappy world with dignity. He was still an officer and also descended from a royal line.

But at the penultimate moment, his courage and his faith both deserted him. He scrabbled for a hold on the pavement and tried to crawl away. A sob escaped him.

A sudden blinding light exploded in the alley and Tran instinctively closed his eyes against the glare. He could still hear too clearly the sound of bullets dancing along the alley toward him. As the first of the hot metal slugs hit Tran's legs, his bladder released.

The line of lead moved up and down his body once, twice, again. Through it all, Tran kept his eyes closed and so denied himself even the small satisfaction of knowing who his killers were.

1

It was the third straight day of rain, not the usual order of things in December, and the squad room had taken on a faint and persistent odor of damp. The effect, wetness mingling uneasily with the ordinary smells of the detective enclave, was not pleasant.

At least, in honor of the season, an attempt had been made to add a little cheer to the surroundings. Someone had kindly installed a small plastic Christmas tree in one corner of the room. It was adorned, although that word seemed misapplied here, with seven purple Styrofoam balls, three clumps of tinsel, and a pair of handcuffs. The weight of the cuffs bent the undersized tree dangerously leeward. On top, the traditional angel had been replaced by an upside-down Dixie cup. There were no gifts around the base of the tree, only a crumpled McDonald's bag.

Blue Maguire scowled at the tree once more. This had been a very long morning, filled almost entirely with overdue reports that had to be written. He didn't mind the typing so much, but the effort involved in trying to decipher the scrawl his partner called handwriting (another instance of a word sadly misapplied) was wearing on both the eyes and the nerves.

It might have eased the chore a little at least if Spaceman Kowalski himself had been present to interpret and also to provide a target for Blue's increasing hostility. Unfortunately, Kowalski had taken the day off to deal with some family business.

Families, Blue thought bitterly, were a pain in the butt. He was probably very lucky not to have one cluttering up his landscape.

"I'm looking for a guy named Maguire."

The slightly nasal female voice broke into his petulant reverie. He looked up from the page of hieroglyphics he was laboring over. "I'm Detective Maguire," he admitted.

His first impression was one of youth—an impression he seemed to receive from others more often with each passing day. Straight hair that fell below her shoulders, faded tight jeans, and a Mötley Crüe teeshirt all combined to make him think that the woman was young.

She gestured vaguely toward the stairs. "They told me down there that I should talk to you."

"Pull up a chair." He had a headache and was feeling distinctly unsociable, but after all, he was a civil servant. And at the moment, even dealing with a member of the great unwashed public beat ruining his baby blues over Kowalski's damned chicken scratches any longer.

As she sat, he had the chance to take a better look and to realize that his initial impression had been wrong. The woman was older than he'd thought and than she wanted to be. In her late twenties, probably, with makeup applied sloppily and too thickly in a vain attempt to hide the lines beginning to show.

His gaze seemed to make her nervous. She reached for and lit a cigarette, exhaling a cloud of smoke across the space between them.

Perfect, Blue thought, wearily waving it away. Just what the room needed. One of these days he really was going to hang a "No Smoking" sign over his desk, instead of just threatening to do so. He wasn't entirely convinced that Spaceman would then follow up on his threat to move his adjoining desk out into the hall.

"What can I do for you, Miss—?"

"Wexler. Marybeth."

"What's the problem, Miss Wexler?"

"This guy I'm living with is up to something."

Terrific. Being up to something was a second class felony in the state. Blue was really getting ticked off at his partner for choosing this day to disappear. "Like what?"

She looked mildly annoyed at his stupidity. "How am I supposed to know what? I'm not a cop. But he acts real suspicious."

Well, that was only a misdemeanor.

His headache was getting worse. Blue leaned both elbows on the edge of the desk and massaged his temples. What the devil had he said or done lately that would make the desk sergeant mad enough to send this particular fruitcake up here? "Could you be just a little more specific?"

The brow furrowed. "What?"

"Let's start off with something easy. What's the man's name?"

"Wolf."

"Wolf? That's it?"

"Yeah." She removed the cigarette from her mouth long enough to gnaw a bit of nail from one finger. "At least, that's what he calls himself." She brightened as an idea struck. "Maybe it's like a nickname or something."

"Maybe. How long have you known him?"

"A week. A week yesterday."

His thought about the great unwashed public had been more or less a joke, but now Blue noticed a faint ring of grime around Wexler's neck. Maybe she had just showered too quickly this morning. And every other morning for the past six months or so. "A week? And you're living with him?"

She stared at him for a moment, then shrugged. "You never heard of love at first sight?"

He realized with some surprise that she was making a joke.

"Besides, it's not really like we're living together. We're just both staying in the same place. Cheaper that way."

"Uh-huh. Has Wolf actually done anything illegal?"

"Maybe. Probably. How do I know? He keeps going out at weird times. And he's all the time making phone calls."

"To whom?"

"I don't know to whom, because he makes me leave the room, even if I'm right in the middle of a television show. Why would he do that, unless he's up to something?"

"Maybe he has a wife."

Scratching idly at some point just below her left breast, she considered that briefly. Then she shook her head. "Nope. Not this guy. He's too damned wild to have a wife."

"Wild?"

Marybeth Wexler shifted in the chair, wriggling thoughtfully. "I don't mean he like boozes a lot or does drugs. Not that kind of wild. Wolf is just different than any guy I knew before." She looked for an ashtray on his desk, didn't see one, and crushed out the butt under the four-inch spike heel of her shoe. "Wolf is real quiet. He don't say much at all, and even when he does, his voice is soft. You get what I mean?" She waved a hand helplessly. "He's like an animal. Quiet and real sneaky."

"Okay. But you still haven't told me about any crime this man might have committed."

"No, but—"

Blue shrugged. "Then I'm afraid there's nothing I can do. Nothing the police department can do."

She was silent, staring past him at the Christmas tree. "I think he might kill me," she whispered finally, the words almost swallowed up by the noise of the squad room.

"Kill you?" Blue didn't want this. They already had enough dead bodies littering up their caseload. "Why do you think that? Has he threatened you? Or hurt you?"

Across the room, someone laughed loudly and suddenly. She was startled by the noise. When her attention returned to Blue, she chewed on her lower lip for a moment. "No, nothing like that. But sometimes when he looks at me, I get scared. His eyes are a funny color. Like cold steel." She was spitting the words out machine-gun style. "He can give you a chill just by looking at you. Like when somebody walks over your grave."

Blue occasionally got fed up with how stupid people could be. It made him tired just trying to deal with them. "Why don't you just leave?" he said.

"Leave?"

"Miss Wexler, you've known this man for only a week. You claim he's up to something illegal, and most of all, you're afraid of him. So why the hell don't you just split?"

The expression on her face gave him the impression that she had never even considered that option. "Well," she said slowly, "maybe I could do that. But I think it might be a good idea to wait until after Christmas. It's the pits to be by yourself over the holidays. Especially since I've got no place else to go. And sometimes Wolf is okay. He gives me a little money. And he's good in the sack. At least, he was the first couple days. Now, he don't seem to care about that no more. He's stopped screwing me. So it's almost like a little vacation." She took a deep breath, then exhaled slowly. "Hell's bells, I guess a broad would have to be crazy to walk out on a deal like that, right?"

Blue shook his head slightly. "Whatever you say."

She stood, smoothing the front of the garish teeshirt. The prissy gesture seemed almost comically incongruous when contrasted with the rest of the picture she presented. "So, I guess it's thanks anyway."

Blue stared at her. "You be careful," he said.

She grinned suddenly, a surprisingly good-humored and attractive smile. "I've been careful for a long time," she said. "It's a way of life for some of us."

Blue smiled too, though not really at her. "For all of us, Miss Wexler."

She nodded and turned to leave, her heels making sharp

little clicks on the floor. Blue watched until she was out of sight, then picked up the report he'd been working on before the interruption. By the time the sound of her footsteps faded, he'd forgotten Marybeth Wexler.

2

The Little Saigon Café was on Third Street, tucked pre-
cariously between a synthetic wig shop patronized primarily
by hookers and transvestites, and a storefront Buddhist temple. The temple belonged to an obscure sect, mostly Americans, leftover weirdos from the 1960s.

Lars Morgan parked the rent-a-heap brown Ford, perfect
in its blandness, across the street from the café. There were
no pedestrians on the sidewalks, except one young and very
drunk Hispanic man who had paused to urinate against the
side of the temple. Whether his action was a religious state-
ment or merely the result of a full bladder wasn't clear.

The rain had stopped, for the moment at least. Instead of
getting out of the car immediately, though, Lars lit a Gitane
and sat where he was, staring through the dirty windshield
at the small stucco building.

It wasn't exactly nerves that kept him sitting there. More
like anticipation. Over the years, Lars had created, not without pain, a philosophy to live by: Life was much like a chess
game. It was a trite way to think and he knew that, but it was
also useful because it kept him careful. He had learned his
chess in a jail cell in some emerging African nation that he
could no longer remember the name of. If it even had the
same name now, which he doubted.

Essentially, the game appealed to him because of its sense
of order. He liked that. Planning and strategy were para-

mount to him, so he never liked to rush his next move, even when he knew exactly what that move was going to be. Part of the pleasure in life was to savor these quiet moments. It was like foreplay, kind of. The comparison made him smile.

When the cigarette was gone, he flicked the butt out into the gutter almost jauntily. Time for the White Knight to make his opening move.

The drunk had finished peeing and was now making his erratic way toward Alameda. He'd forgotten to close his fly. More important, as far as Lars was concerned, he didn't seem to take any notice at all of a man getting out of his car and carefully locking the door. With crime the way it was these days, it made no sense to take chances.

As Lars crossed Third and headed toward the café, he ran one hand through his dark blond hair. Getting shaggy, he realized, time to visit the frigging stylist again. And whatever had happened to plain old barbers?

Closeup, the Little Saigon was clearly a dump. This was not where the beautiful people of Los Angeles came to satisfy their faddish taste for Vietnamese cuisine. A hand-lettered sign in the front window apologized for the fact that the place was closed and invited the prospective customer to return at another time. Lars couldn't imagine anyone bothering to come here once, never mind twice.

Despite the sign, when Lars turned the knob, the door swung open. A tinny bell sounded a warning as he stepped inside. He closed the door again, reaching back with one hand to slide the lock into place. The small click it made gave him a feeling of security. This deal was getting to the point where he needed somebody around to cover his ass. Soon.

The powerful smells inside hit him like a physical blow. The aromas seemed at once familiar and exotic and the sensation made him a little dizzy.

"You're late." A short, wiry man just past middle age and wrapped in a big white apron appeared in the room.

Lars moved toward the small bar, automatically reaching for another cigarette. "Tough shit," he muttered. "What difference does it make? You got something more important to do with your time?"

"I have got a business to run." Hua's English was still heavily accented.

Lars glanced around the grimy café. "And the place seems to be flourishing," he said.

Hua either did not catch the sarcasm or simply chose to ignore it. "I get along. Now I belong to the Chamber of Commerce."

"Glad to hear it. Things like that sort of prove that this is still the land of golden fucking opportunity." Lars slid onto a stool. "Gimme a beer."

"On the house or will you pay?"

"I'll pay, damnit." People never changed; Hua was still the same bastard he'd been as a government lackey in Saigon.

Hua reached into a large stainless steel cooler, then slid a bottle of beer down the bar toward him. The brand was one Lars had never heard of. "This thing is making me nervous," Hua said.

"You were always nervous." Lars took a long gulp of the beer, letting the overchilled liquid soothe his dry smoker's throat. It had a terrible taste. "You were always a chickenshit coward, in fact."

Hua did not seem to take umbrage at the remark; he was a man who long ago lost the freedom to feel offended by anything that was said to him, at least by certain men. He just reached into the cooler again, this time pulling out a bottle of Ripple. Ignoring Lars's snort of derision, he poured himself a glassful.

Lars set his beer down carefully. "I believe that you have some information to give me?"

"To sell you."

Lars conceded that with a one-shoulder shrug.

Hua was staring into the wine, apparently looking for some secret he thought was contained there. He spoke without raising his eyes. "This is not a wise thing we are doing, Morgan."

"What does that mean?"

"There are dangerous men involved."

Lars raised a brow. "I'm a dangerous man, Hua. You should remember that."

He could not have forgotten the old days, when the two of them worked on the Interrogation Squad. There was always information that some bigshot thought was important, and Lars Morgan was the best there was at getting that information out of the prisoners. He was the best, despite the fact that the job wasn't really to his taste. Combat suited him much more.

Hua smiled faintly. "I have not forgotten. You were tough and efficient. But, Lieutenant Morgan, you are a soldier. That is all you have ever been, whether you wear the famous beret and represent the American government, or whether you simply offer yourself to the highest bidder. You have the heart and soul of a soldier."

Lars was bored. "So fucking what?"

"The rules are different here, old friend. The men who you would challenge now are not soldiers. They are thugs and gangsters."

"Is that supposed to scare me off?"

"Perhaps."

"Well, it doesn't."

"Then you are more of a fool than I thought."

He felt a rush of heat to his face. To hell with this. The little bastard had no right to be calling him names.

But Lars fought down the surge of anger. He never allowed himself the luxury of that emotion. It had no place on the chessboard, because it could lead to mistakes. He couldn't afford any blunders at this point. He swallowed once, then smiled. "What do you have for me, Hua?"

After a moment, the other man shrugged, as if to wash his hands of any further responsibility for what might happen. He reached into the cooler one more time and pulled out a small plastic bag. Inside the bag, Lars could see a key. Without speaking, Hua walked out from behind the bar and disappeared into the kitchen.

Lars drank the rest of the beer, making a face at the horse-piss taste. He took out his cotton handkerchief and wiped all sides of the bottle, then the edge of the bar where his fingers might accidentally have rested. He worked carefully, methodically, and when he was done, he refolded the now damp square of cloth and put it into his pocket again. He could get the door on the way out.

He slid one hand inside his denim jacket to unsnap the top of his shoulder holster quietly. His fingers touched the famil-iar cold steel reassuringly.

So Hua thought he was stupid? Well, that little prick would find out soon enough who was the fool. Lars smiled at his reflection in the dusty mirror behind the bar. He straight-ened his collar. Things were going much more smoothly than he had expected. And tomorrow it would get better, when he made contact with his friends.

The kitchen door swung open and Hua came back, carry-ing a manila envelope. Lars shifted his shoulders slightly inside the jacket and swiveled on the stool to face Hua. He was still smiling.

Hua saw the smile. He stopped suddenly and stared at Lars. Oh yes, the little creep remembered the old days.

3

Spaceman Kowalski reached for a cigarette.

Then he saw the sign. Its message was firm, verging on outright hostility, and the point was made effectively. With a sigh, he pulled his hand back. The world could be a very unfriendly place these days, especially for a nicotine junkie.

Across the rather dismal dayroom, two boys were playing a game of Ping-Pong. The match was so spiritless that it seemed to be happening in slow motion. Spaceman wondered if they were doped up or just too damned lazy to move any faster.

In the corner, a group was gathered around a flickering television screen watching "Sesame Street." Oscar the Grouch was explaining all about the letter W. Although the boys in front of the set were in their teens, they seemed to be listening with interest.

Spaceman wished that good old Oscar could explain why he was here. Why his son, *his* son for Chrissake, was being kept in this place.

Tell me, Oscar old buddy, just how the devil can life get so totally screwed up?

He played absently with his red Bic lighter and after a moment, a faint smile appeared on his face. Not, after all, totally screwed up. There was Lainie. She was the best part of his life right now. Otherwise, there wasn't much beyond trouble with this kid, hassles with his ex-wife, and the job, always the job. He liked being a cop, loved his work in fact, but at the same time he knew that the job was wearing him down, eroding him. But having Lainie as a part of his life made up for a lot.

The door finally opened and Robbie came into the room. He was institutional pale, like a con in the joint, and painfully thin. The blue jeans and white teeshirt he wore hung on his body as if they belonged to someone else. In one hand he carried a red nylon duffel bag and in the other, a windbreaker.

Robbie walked to the center of the room and stopped, just standing there.

"Hi, there, Son," Spaceman said.

"Hi."

"All set?"

"Yeah, sure." He glanced around the room vaguely, as if there might be something he'd forgotten. Then he shrugged. "I'm ready."

"Let's hit the road, then." His cheeriness sounded phony even to him.

But they couldn't go quite yet. There were some formalities to be taken care of before they could escape the dreary surroundings of the hospital. They stopped at the front desk, where Spaceman signed a sheaf of official and officious-looking papers. He promised, among other things, to return Robert Allan Kowalski to the custody of the youth authority not later than noon on the second of January. He also guaranteed that the aforementioned minor would be under properly constituted parental authority throughout the holiday leave.

Robbie stood to one side, apparently more interested in memorizing the fading checkerboard pattern on the linoleum floor than in the administrative details of his temporary release. He stayed quiet even as they were finally able to leave the old brick building and head for the car.

Once behind the wheel, Spaceman reached immediately for the cigarette he'd been craving and lit it. After a brief hesitation, he offered the pack to Robbie. The boy took one, nodding his thanks. They both inhaled gratefully.

Spaceman started the car, listening to the engine grind, hoping they would make it back to the city. "Bet you're glad to be going home for a while, huh?"

Robbie was quiet for such a long time that Spaceman almost repeated the question. Finally Robbie spoke. "Yeah. Sure. Why not?"

As he drove from the hospital grounds and turned south on 101, Spaceman tried to think of something else to say. But as usual when he was with his son, nothing came to mind.

It was Robbie who finally broke the silence. "Can I turn the radio on?"

"I guess so."

He played with the dial for several static-cluttered minutes, finally settling on a station that played only the golden oldies of rock and roll. The sound of "I Can't Get No Satisfaction" blasted into the car.

Spaceman wondered bleakly when the devil his own life had become just a subject for nostalgia. It made him feel old. He also felt guilty about having the radio on when he knew that they should be talking—although he sure as hell didn't know what they should be talking about—but it was easier just to let the music take over.

And besides, it was no big deal. Just the latest failure in sixteen years of haphazard fatherhood.

Later, he promised himself, later they would talk, get through the stone wall that seemed to keep them apart.

For now, he just settled down for the drive, taking long drags on the cigarette and wondering what his partner was up to. Maybe when they stopped for lunch, he'd call, just to check.

4

It was late by the time he finally got back to the motel in West Hollywood and parked the old Ford between a rusting van and the Army-green trash bin. This spot was his favorite for parking, because it was hard to see from the street. Lars liked to keep a low profile.

The hallway was empty as he climbed the one flight of stairs to his room. More than just a room, actually, because it also had a kitchenette and a small living area separate from the bedroom. This motel had been his home for just over a week now; its chief advantage was the low rates. He was getting tired of the air of grim depression in the place, however. The peeling paint and subtle stink of greasy food and human debris that clung tenaciously to the very walls seemed drearily like so many of the dumps he'd lived in over the years.

But soon he'd be able to kiss off this kind of life for good. Before much longer, he'd be living like a fucking Arab sheik.

Lars thought with mild regret about the money he no doubt could have taken from Hua. But the idea repelled him somehow, in the same way he had always viewed with distaste the looting and sacking of enemy villages during any of the wars he'd been in. Kill the bastards, burn the huts, whatever duty required, but for Chrissake, a soldier didn't pick the bones of his victims. Not a warrior. And to steal the money from Hua would have been no different. Lars Morgan wasn't a thief. He just wanted what was rightfully his.

Still, he sighed a bit regretfully.

The broad was sitting in her usual corner of the couch, which made him sigh again. He had been harboring a small hope that maybe she'd left during the day. But no such luck. God, he was tired of her, but at the moment, he was so wrapped up in other things, important things, that it was too much trouble to bother dumping her. But soon.

She barely glanced up from Johnny Carson as he came in. "About time," she said.

Ignoring the comment, he stood behind the closet door to take off his jacket and holster. Wouldn't you think she'd get the message? Hell, he hadn't even touched her in days. He looped the holster over a coat hook and draped the denim jacket over it.

"You want supper?"

"I ate already."

She looked indignant. "Well, hell, you might have let me know before I went to all that trouble."

He sat in the tattered recliner, leaning forward briefly to unlace his boots. "All what trouble?" Usually her idea of making an effort was running down to the chink's on the corner for some lukewarm chow mein.

"I made a meat loaf. It's keeping warm in the oven, but it's probably all dried out by now. Thanks to you."

"Fuck your meat loaf."

"Well, fuck you, too." She picked up a bottle of beer and took a gulp.

They both seemed to get bored with the conversation at the same time. Lars leaned back and closed his eyes. The day had been long and not very productive. Hua's information, while moderately interesting, had proved much less helpful than anticipated. Sometimes it seemed like he took two steps back for every one ahead.

He stretched. God, he was looking forward to seeing the

guys again. This Lone Ranger routine was wearing on the nerves.

"Wolf, let's go dancing, huh? It's early yet." She inhaled noisily on one of the low quality joints she always had.

Lars wished that she would just shut the hell up. Women. More trouble than they were worth. He liked it when a broad knew enough to show up just when he wanted to screw and then disappear again.

He willed Wexler to vanish.

But she didn't. Her voice just went on and on.

Suddenly something she said registered. Slowly he lowered the recliner until his feet were flat on the floor again. He opened his eyes and stared at her.

She seemed to realize her mistake; he noticed for the first time how stoned she really was, which explained the stupid thing she'd just said.

Lars didn't speak for a long time, and when he did, the words came out almost in a whisper. "What did you say?"

"Nothing, Wolf, I didn't say nothing important." She wriggled, as if trying to squeeze herself right into the worn nubby surface of the couch.

"Damnit, don't lie to me, you bitch. You said something about the cops."

She just shook her head.

Lars didn't let himself explode. Instead, he just leaned back in the chair again and closed his eyes. It was easier to think that way.

Wexler, the stupid whore, must have decided that everything was okay again. She stayed quiet, apparently engrossed once more in the television. Once she giggled softly at something Ed McMahon said.

Lars knew that it was time, past time, for Marybeth Wexler to disappear from his life. Permanently.

The decision made, he relaxed.

5

Blue was so tired that the green, perfectly balanced Porsche traveled the winding road home more through pure mechanical instinct than anything he did. When he finally had the car parked safely in the driveway, he let out a sigh and sat still for a moment before summoning up the energy to get out.

He called softly for Merlin, but the cat seemed to be nowhere around. Probably out getting a little from one of the female felines in the neighborhood. It was a sad state of affairs when a man's cat had a better sex life than he did.

The mailbox was jammed full of envelopes. Blue took all of them inside and dropped the bundle on the couch, forgetting it while he kicked off his shoes, removed tie and gun, and then poured himself a glass of Glen Livet over a couple of ice cubes. Automatically, he switched on his Bearcat scanner, more for the noise it provided than out of any burning need to know what was happening in the city on this particular night. Just before sitting down on the sofa with the mail, he pulled open the drapes that covered the vast picture window.

Below was the city. From up here, where the monied and lucky lived, Los Angeles at night was a blanket of glittering lights and promised wonders. Blue was not so tired that he didn't feel the usual sense of gratitude for the fact of his rich father. The old man had been a genuine bastard while alive, but his death made up for all of that by making his only son and heir a millionaire several times over.

Of all the good things his money allowed him to have, Blue thought that this view was the most precious. Even though he knew full well that the glitter was mostly fool's gold and the promises were mostly lies, he could still get a good feeling looking down at his city.

Blue took a long drink of the Scotch, letting its warmth and smoothness soothe him, loosen the tight muscles. Only then did he reach for the first envelope. It was a Christmas card, but the names embossed inside in gold meant nothing to him at all. He dropped both the card and the envelope into the wastebasket. Several more cards received the same fate in rapid succession.

He knew that all these people who sent the expensive, impersonal cards were former friends and business associates of the old man's. What he couldn't understand was why the hell, all these years later, they were still sending him season's greetings. Probably they all figured that sooner or later he'd get tired of playing cops and robbers and take direct control over the vast computer empire founded by Hank Maguire. When that happened, nobody wanted to be on junior's shitlist. So they sent him Christmas cards and frequent invitations to fancy parties.

The attitude annoyed him and even seemed to diminish him in some way. He was a cop, damnit, and that was what he wanted to be, all he wanted to be. More than just a public relations hack, too, now that he was in homicide. That meant he was good.

He poured another drink.

One of the cards was from Lieutenant McGannon and his ever-increasing brood. That one, instead of being pitched, was carefully propped on the table, where a few others, also mostly from fellow cops, already stood.

By the time he was through the pile of mail, Blue had finished a second drink and poured another, not bothering with ice this time. He thought blearily that probably some food would be a good idea, but the effort involved seemed too great, so he sat where he was, watching the lights and listening to the radio while he sipped.

When the phone rang, he jumped, startled out of the half-sleep that had wrapped around him. He set the drink safely out of the way and reached for the receiver. "H'lo?"

"This Blue Maguire?"

"Yes." He shook his head slightly to clear the fog and erase the confusion. When he got a call at this hour, he always assumed that it was Spaceman. That this time it wasn't his partner muddled him a little. "Who's this?"

"Oh, you probably don't remember me. That don't matter. I just wanted to call and see how you're doing. So, how're you doing, old buddy?"

The voice rang no immediate bells with Blue. Male, not young and not old, maybe edged a little with booze, but then so was his. "I'm doing fine, but I don't talk to anonymous callers."

"At least you're still alive. That's good. I was afraid you might be dead." The voice sounded sad. "A lot of people are dead now."

Blue hung up.

He was shaking a little, not from fear, but from bewilderment. Weariness and alcohol made his mind feel numb, and the unknown voice talking about death had rattled him.

He reached for the glass again, then stopped himself.

Damnit to hell, he had to stop this. Too much booze lately, too many missed meals. Not enough exercise. Those were all bad signs. A lot of cops ended up in a pool of alcohol. Well, it wasn't going to happen to Blue Maguire.

He took the glass to the kitchen and rinsed it out carefully. Then he picked up his discarded shoes, tie and jacket, and holster, and climbed the circular staircase to his bedroom.

6

"This is shit."

Spaceman snapped closed the file on Sister Maria Dominic and tossed it toward Blue's desk. It hit against a paper cup sitting there. The cup tilted, hung suspended for a fleeting moment, then gave up and fell on its side, spreading a sticky pool of Tab over everything in sight.

Blue jumped back just before the unrelenting wave of soda reached the edge of the desk and dripped onto his new white jeans. He grabbed a handful of tissues and tried hopelessly to clean up the mess. "Thanks a lot, you bastard," he muttered.

Spaceman glanced up, surprised to notice the disaster. "Sorry about that," he said absently.

"Damn." Blue aimed the sodden wad of Kleenex in the general direction of the wastebasket and stalked out of the squad room.

Spaceman watched him go, slightly bewildered. His partner, usually the mildest of men, with a disposition so even that it could get a little boring, had been in a sour mood all morning. Something was bugging the guy and now Blue seemed to be blaming him for the fact that this case, which they'd been busting ass over for almost two weeks now, was still garbage.

And while Spaceman was willing to admit that everyone was entitled to an off day every now and again, it really wasn't quite kosher for a man's partner all of a sudden to start doing a Jekyll and Hyde on him.

"Kowalski!" A familiar deep voice rumbled through the squad room.

He groaned silently. Damn. Just what he needed at this exact moment, a chewing out from McGannon. He and Blue had successfully dodged the boss for several days now, but apparently that streak of good luck was over.

By the time Spaceman reached the lieutenant's office, McGannon was already settled again behind his massive oak desk. His square phallic symbol somebody once called it. Behind McGannon's back, of course.

"You rang, sir?" Spaceman said, dropping heavily into a chair.

"When was that suit last pressed?" McGannon said sourly.

"Couple months ago. Too much pressing weakens the threads, you know."

McGannon snorted.

"Besides, we have a deal, Maguire and I. He looks good and I think good. It works."

McGannon shrugged to indicate that he was done with small talk. "What the devil is going on around here?"

"Not much," Spaceman replied cheerfully.

The lieutenant played with a letter opener that was a miniature Samurai sword. He looked like the idea of plunging the blade into the heart of a certain homicide detective was beginning to sound good.

Spaceman took a deep breath. It was sort of amazing the way his damned partner always managed to absent himself at times like this. "Well," he said. "We have five working homicides."

"If it wouldn't be too much trouble, could you give me a status report? Just to satisfy my own unreasonable sense of curiosity, you understand."

It was hard to believe that a man who kept pictures of all his kids and his apparently permanently pregnant wife in his office could speak so sarcastically.

Spaceman held up a fist. "The liquor store clerk was shotgunned by a couple of underage punks because he wouldn't sell them a bottle of two-dollar whiskey. We are attempting to locate said punks from a description given by a very satisfied and very drunk customer of the store, who happened to be sitting on the curb when the shooting came down. According to him, both boys were black—but not real black—of average height and weight, with moderate Afros. Blue and I are scouring the city for two young males who fit that description." He raised one finger from the fist.

McGannon snorted. "I'll light a candle for you."

"Thanks very much. To continue: The doper in the alley set himself on fire, in our expert opinion." Finger two came up. "The woman on Wilshire was axed by somebody she picked up in a bar. Unfortunately, since her livelihood was, in fact, picking men up in bars, we have a wide field of suspects."

"A hooker," McGannon said distastefully. He did not approve of prostitutes; in fact, he frowned on anything that served to erode the almighty Catholic family structure.

"But still a victim," Spaceman reminded him, wondering how a man with such a fastidious sense of morality had survived as a cop. Two fingers were still lowered. "We don't have much on the mugger who knifed the French sightseer."

"I'd like to see you wrap that one up."

"Yes, I know, so would the Chamber of Commerce, I'm sure. Bad for the tourist business." The thumb came up slowly. "We have absolutely nowhere to go on that nun killing."

McGannon didn't even want to talk about that case. Spaceman didn't know if he was more bothered by the fact of the old nun's bloody death or by the evidence that she had been repeatedly raped in the process.

He closed his hand into a fist again. "That's our caseload."

McGannon swiveled in his chair. After several moments, he made a gesture both disgusted and dismissive. "Dump

the doper case," he said. "Put the hooker and the liquor
store clerk on the back burner."

"Sure thing; they'll never know the difference."

"Concentrate on the nun and the French guy." McGannon gave him a deathmask smile. "Until something new
comes in. Then you can concentrate on that."

"Thank you." Spaceman, figuring that the meeting was
over, pushed himself up from the chair and started for the
door.

"It's been about six months now, right?" McGannon said
suddenly. "How's this Maguire working out?"

Spaceman paused, wondering where the question was
coming from. What did it really signify? Office politics were
a quagmire he tried to avoid. "He's okay," was all he said
and that was said carefully.

"Maybe he belongs back on the public relations lunch
circuit." It was almost a question the way McGannon said it.

Spaceman opened the door. "Why make waves?" he said.
"Maguire is okay. We get along. We break the cases,
usually. When they can be broken."

McGannon nodded. "If you say so."

Spaceman stepped out of the office, carefully closing the
door. It occurred to him that he'd just blown the chance to
rid himself of Maguire and be a free agent again. The
thought bemused him a little.

Then he realized: What the hell? He was used to the guy.
Better the devil you know, his father always said. Maguire
was okay.

Blue was back at his desk, just hanging up the phone, as
Spaceman returned. "Don't bother sitting down," Blue said
shortly. "We're rolling."

Spaceman didn't even take the time to ask what was going
on. It didn't matter. He just reached into the drawer for his
gun and shoved it into the holster. As they headed out the
door, Spaceman thought about McGannon's smile and the
prediction of a new case.

The son of a bitch had put an Irish curse on him.

By the time they arrived, the Little Saigon Café seemed to be filled with blue uniforms. By actual count, there weren't that many officers inside, but the place was small, and anyway, it didn't take too many hulking cops to make a crowd. Spaceman cringed, thinking about what all those hands and feet might be doing to any evidence at the scene.

The group quieted when he and Blue entered. "What the devil is this?" Spaceman said in a loud voice. "A frigging union meeting? Get the hell out of here, everybody except the ones who made the call."

There was a general move toward the door, along with some muttered comments about hotshot homicide dicks. Two cops stayed behind, apparently the ones who had found the body.

The body in question was sprawled on the floor in back of the bar. He was—or had been anyway—a small man, Oriental, wearing dark slacks and a white apron. Whatever he had been, he was now nothing more than an object of mild curiosity.

As they took all that in, one of the zone-car cops stepped forward. She was bright-faced and eager, flipping open her notebook with crisp efficiency. "His name was Hua," she said crisply. This here was a broad with her sights set on a gold shield, no doubt about it. "He was the owner of this place. Death, by my guess, occurred sometime late yesterday."

"Is that your guess?" Spaceman said dryly. "Terrific. You won't mind if we check that with the medical examiner, will you?"

"No, sir." She glanced at the notebook again. "Cause of death apparently was a single gunshot to the back of the head. Execution style." She said the last two words with relish.

Spaceman glanced at her partner, an old-timer, whose name he couldn't remember. "You concur with all that?"

The grey-haired man shrugged. "Why not?"

She looked as if there might be more she wanted to say,

but Spaceman turned away before she got the chance. As he knelt beside the body for a closer look, Blue checked out the bar. He picked up a menu and began to read. "Damn," he said to no one in particular. "Seeing this makes me hungry for some of the food I had in Nam. Hell, he even has *heo ram sot ca cha gio.*"

Spaceman straightened. "I never got into that stuff much."

"I expect not," Blue said wryly. "No catsup. What's this look like? Robbery?"

"If so, the perp screwed up. The stiff has a nice wad of bills in his pocket."

"Maybe something scared him off."

Spaceman shrugged. "Maybe. But if somebody came along and saw what was happening, why didn't we find out before now?"

Blue had no answer for that. He tossed the menu onto the bar, ignoring the glare of a labman who was trying to get some prints, and leaned forward to peer at the empty beer bottle sitting there. "Christ, if Hua was serving somebody this stuff, no wonder he got killed. I'd call that justifiable homicide."

Before Spaceman could respond, the door opened again and Sharon Engels came in. "Nice of the medical examiner's office to show up at our party," he said.

Sharon saw them and smiled faintly.

Blue nodded at her.

Spaceman watched the cool exchange curiously. "Trouble in paradise?" he asked under his breath.

All he got was a bland gaze from his partner, a look that gave away absolutely nothing. Spaceman grinned and then turned his attention back to the dead man.

7

Lars found the building he was looking for without any difficulty: Addison Gallery. A few tasteful prints were on display behind the shining front window. Lars was impressed. A classy building on the money end of Wilshire Boulevard. That bastard Conway was doing pretty good for himself.

He ran a hand through his hair to remove some of the tangles and buttoned the collar of his faded khaki shirt. Underdressed, for damned sure, but it couldn't be helped. His schedule had been thrown slightly out of whack because he'd been forced to deal with the problem of the dumb broad, Wexler, sooner and more drastically than he'd intended. Now, not willing to risk staying in the motel and maybe facing questions about his missing roommate, he was living temporarily in the Ford. That made it hard to stay real tidy. At least, he'd shaved in the restroom of the gas station before coming here.

Luck seemed to be with him, because he had just the right change for the parking meter. The rental heap looked even worse than ever, surrounded by all the Mercedeses and Caddys cluttering the street.

According to the calligraphic sign on the door the gallery wouldn't open for another hour, but he never believed what he read, and sure enough, the door opened.

Inside, everything was beige and ivory. Two of the walls

were bare, awaiting an offering, but the others were dotted with photographs, all of which seemed to be of poor people someplace. He gave them a quick look, then ignored them.

It was much harder to ignore the ivory and beige woman who appeared as if by magic in front of him. Lars gazed at her in silent admiration. He was six feet tall, and she had a good two inches on him. The simple sand-colored suit she wore, with no blouse under the buttoned jacket, set off the whole length of her tanned body perfectly.

Lars wondered just what a man had to do in his life to get a chance at screwing a broad like this. It would no doubt be worth a couple extra years in purgatory for just one shot at her. Then it occurred to him that having a lot of money was probably the first prerequisite—this bitch wasn't going to spread her legs for guy living in a rented Ford, for Chrissake—and that realization reminded him of his mission here.

The woman, meanwhile, seemed to be waiting patiently for him to collect his thoughts. She was probably used to having this effect on men. "I'm sorry," she said finally, softly, "but the gallery isn't open yet."

"I know that, honey. I'm looking for Devlin Conway. He's supposed to be having some kind of show here, right?"

"Mr. Conway's photography exhibition opens in a few days", she said. "But it happens that he is here now, talking with Mr. Addison about the arrangements."

This was great. He'd hoped these people could tell him where to find Conway, and instead he'd found the man himself. Lars was only ordinarily superstitious, but he chose to view this break as a good omen. "I need to see Conway," he said.

"This isn't usual. . . ."

He dug his heels into the thick ivory carpet and waited. She sighed. "Who shall I say is asking for him?"

Lars flashed a grin in her direction. "Just an old friend."

Still looking doubtful, she nevertheless sat down at the desk and picked up the receiver of the ivory phone. "Mr.

Addison? I'm very sorry to disturb you, sir, but there's a . . . gentleman out here who insists on seeing Mr. Conway. An old friend who won't give his name."

Behind the polished smoothness of her voice, Lars could hear a slight tension. She didn't quite know what she was dealing with here—an innocent, albeit slightly uncouth visitor, or a genuine Los Angeles nutcase. To put her at ease, he smiled and began a slow tour of the gallery, whistling softly.

She replaced the phone and busied herself, or pretended to, with some papers on the desk.

It was a few more minutes before a door at the back of the gallery opened. "Yes, what is it?" The voice sounded brusque and irritable, but it was unmistakable: You could take the boy out of Australia's sticks, but he was still an Aussie.

Lars turned around. "Mr. Conway, how the hell are you?"

Devlin stared for a moment, his mouth hanging open. "You bastard," he said finally.

The broad looked from one to the other, still not quite sure what was going on.

"Smile when you call me that," Lars said, grinning.

Devlin seemed to recover from the immediate shock and took control of the situation. Shortly, they were alone in Addison's office. Addison himself, a tweedy man with thin lips and a nervous twitch, stayed out front with the broad.

When the door was closed, Devlin turned to look at him. "You bastard," he said again. Then he stepped closer and they embraced tightly. Letting go, Devlin walked behind the desk to sit in the plush leather swivel chair. Lars sat across from him. "You might let a man hear from you," Devlin said after they'd just looked at one another for a moment.

"I've been busy."

"For three bloody years?"

Lars was genuinely surprised. "Jesus, has it been that long?"

"At least. Hell, I thought you were dead."

"Me? No way, babe. You should know better than that."

Devlin Conway hadn't changed much in those three years. In fact, he still looked pretty much as he had many more years ago than that when they'd first met in Nam. He looked good, the dark hair almost untouched by grey and the lean face still mostly unlined.

"How'd you know where to find me?"

Lars shrugged. "I keep track. Besides, it was in the *Times*. About this show or whatever."

"Whatever is right. My artistic pretensions." He indicated a stack of photos. "We were just making the final decision about which ones to hang."

Lars pulled the photographs closer and began to go through them curiously. Visions of another time and another place rose up to assault him. His baptism of fire. "Stinking little war," he muttered.

"Aren't they all? So what have you been doing since that night in San Diego?"

Lars looked up with a sudden smile. "That night in San Diego. Christ, was I drunk."

"Me, too. And by the time I sobered up, you were gone. Off to Zambia or some place, according to the note."

"Some place."

"You don't happen to remember the name of the broad we took to the hotel with us, do you?"

Lars shook his head. "You must be kidding. Did she even have a name? All I remember is that she cost us three hundred bucks."

"And worth every penny. Best fuck we ever had."

"If you say so. I don't remember that either." He shrugged and got back to the original question. "I've been bouncing around. Africa. Central America. Here and there."

"Looking for more stinking little wars."

"It's a living." His hand, which had still been flipping through the photographs, stopped suddenly. "Shit, that's me."

"Sure. You were there, remember?"

His own image, years younger in actual age and eons younger in experience, started up at him from the stark photo. The soldier was crouched in a watery ditch somewhere north of Saigon, his camouflage fatigues sopping with sweat and stained with blood. His hands were caressing the M-16 like it was a three-hundred dollar whore. A twisted bandana kept the hair out of eyes that gazed directly into the camera. "First picture you took of me."

"Right."

"Remember I couldn't frigging believe it. Look up and see some asshole, clean, with a goddamn crease in his pants, standing there."

Devlin smiled faintly. "The crease didn't last long."

"Nobody told you to jump into the damned ditch with me."

"True."

He was still looking at the face in the picture, as if trying to place it in his memory. "God, I was such a frigging virgin then."

"Oh, I don't know. You seemed pretty tough to me."

"Yeah, well, I thought so, too. Then."

"But you're no innocent anymore, right? Now you're all grown up."

Lars only shrugged. But all of a sudden, he didn't want to look at any more pictures. He shoved them away and settled back in the chair. With deliberation, he withdrew a cigarette and lighted it. He exhaled deeply and gazed at Devlin through the cloud of smoke. "The stones are about to surface."

"The stones?"

"The goddamned diamonds. Our stones, lover boy."

Devlin Conway sat back slowly. "You're joking."

"I never joke about four million dollars."

"How do you know?"

Lars took another drag on the cigarette. "I know." His tone left no doubt about it.

Devlin studied him more closely. "You really are a bastard. You've been waiting for this, haven't you? Ever since the night Tran got wasted and the rocks vanished."

"Of course I've been waiting. I'm just surprised that you haven't been. I mean, four fucking million dollars, Dev." Lars leaned forward eagerly. "You want in?"

"Me?"

"Sure. We were partners back then. Still are, as far as I'm concerned. Besides, this is big. Too damned big for one man to cover."

"Even if that one man is the great Lars Morgan?"

"Even then."

There was a long silence in the room.

Devlin began to swivel back and forth slowly in the chair. It squeaked. "You know, mate, I'm about to take off with this photography thing. Critics, newspapers, the whole damned ballgame. I don't want to fuck up now."

"How can this fuck anything up? You'll be rich enough to buy your own damned gallery. This has nothing to do with your picture taking."

"With what, then?"

Lars crushed out the cigarette. "With our war, maybe."

But Devlin shook his head. "Not my war. All I ever want to know about war anymore is in those photographs. I don't even take pictures of war. Not ever again." His voice grated with a kind of harsh sincerity.

"Call it friendship, then."

"That's not fair."

"Fair?" Lars moved the word around in his mind thoughtfully. "Sorry, but that notion doesn't apply. I want this too much to worry about being sporting or honorable, damnit. Dev, this is my last chance. How much longer can I keep fighting my ass off in every shit-hole of this world? You have this"—he gestured at the room, the pictures—"but I've got nothing, man. Nothing but this one last chance."

Devlin didn't say anything.

Lars sighed. "It's simple: I need you."

He frowned. "What exactly are we up against here?"

"The bad guys," Lars said honestly. "Lots of bad guys."

"That's reassuring."

Lars just looked at him.

Finally Devlin shrugged. "All right. I'm a bloody ass, but all right."

Lars could feel the muscles in his stomach untighten for the first time in days. "Thanks, Dev. I knew you wouldn't let me down. Not you. This is great." He stood. "I'll be in touch."

Devlin looked startled. "That's it? You'll be in touch?"

"Don't sweat it, babe. I've got some arrangements to make." He walked to the door, then stopped. "By the way, do you have any idea where Tobias Reardon is these days? I know he's still in the city, but..."

"Toby? Last I heard, he was still spending a lot of time around the Beverly Wilshire Hotel."

"Oh?"

Devlin smiled. "Toby is the only bastard I ever knew who could make the bitches pay for it and keep coming back for more."

Lars shook his head in silent admiration and left.

Devlin Conway sat where he was, staring at the closed door. He didn't know whether to be scared shitless or excited. This confusion of feelings wasn't new to him; he'd had it before around Lars Morgan. Ever since that first day, in fact, when something he couldn't explain then or now drove him to jump into that damned muddy hole to talk to the grey-eyed young soldier.

Even now, all these years later, he still didn't feel as if he knew the whole truth of Lars Morgan. And this scheme was crazy. Did Lars expect them to just stroll in, take control of all those diamonds, and stroll out again? In Devlin's experience, life was never that simple.

The door opened and Addison came in.

Devlin shoved all thought of Lars and his insane ideas aside for the moment. Hell, for all he knew, Lars might just disappear for three years again. He was one crazy bastard.

8

Spaceman rolled out of bed and padded naked into the bathroom. While he peed and scratched an armpit, he used the time to think about nothing more consequential than how good it felt to scratch and pee. It was a pleasant way to start the day.

Well, he amended, not exactly start. The day had really begun thirty or so minutes before.

When he got back to the bedroom, Lainie was sitting up, wrapped in the sheet. "You're running very late," she said in a slightly hoarse morning voice.

"I worked very late," he said with a shrug. After coughing a couple of times to clear his lungs, he lit a cigarette, then opened a drawer to search for clean shorts and socks. Only his hands searched; his eyes were still on Lainie. Even just awake, with no makeup and her auburn hair a tangled mess, she was still beautiful. Spaceman was mildly surprised every time he woke up and found her in his bed. It didn't happen often enough for his taste.

She was a terrific woman, and most important, a grown woman, not like some of the teenyboppers he'd been with since the divorce. Lainie was smart and funny and sexy.

And she didn't even blame him for getting her brother killed.

Spaceman dismissed that thought immediately.

He finally found some undershorts and began to dress. "Coming back tonight?"

"Can't. This is the Christmas season, in case you forgot. Do you know how much of a bookseller's annual profit comes in December?" Although she had only taken over the bookstore less than six months ago, after Jerry's death, Lainie already sounded like an expert.

"No. How much?"

"A whole lot."

"So when will I see you again?"

"I'll call."

Spaceman tried not to sulk. "Maybe I'll come out to Azusa."

"Fine."

She sounded pleased, but practical. That was good. Who needed a broad swooning and clinging? Still, she might pretend to be a little bit helpless. It occurred to Spaceman that he didn't know what the hell he wanted in a woman.

He finished dressing quickly, kissed her, skipped breakfast, and was waiting, just barely, on the sidewalk—next to his own yet-again disabled car—when the flashy Porsche pulled up.

Blue looked bleary-eyed and uncharacteristically frazzled. Spaceman was startled to notice that his partner hadn't even done a very good job shaving himself. Christ, was the whole world going to hell?

Spaceman lit a cigarette, his third of the morning, and accommodatingly cracked the window open. Nobody would ever be able to say that he didn't go at least halfway in a relationship. "So," he said cheerfully. "How should we go about earning our salaries today?"

Blue shrugged.

"You might show a little more enthusiasm. After all, this job is my life."

"Sorry. I didn't sleep very well."

"Problem?"

"No." The blond hesitated, then shook his head. "I don't think so."

Before Spaceman could decide whether to probe a little deeper into whatever was bugging his partner, the radio crackled and he heard their code number. "Shit, they could at least let us get to the office first," he bitched.

An almost sexless metallic voice gave them an address, along with the cheery news that a dead body awaited their arrival. Spaceman was rapidly losing any inclination to break into Christmas carols.

The address turned out to belong to a long-abandoned gasoline station near Broadway. A squad car was parked rather haphazardly in front, and a small collection of the curious stood on the sidewalk. One of the onlookers was Santa Claus. Things must have been rough up at the old Pole, because Mr. Claus, instead of being jolly and plump, had a distinctly lean and hungry look.

"Ho, ho, ho," Santa said as they walked past. The words floated through the air on a cloud of whiskey fumes.

A uniformed and very fat cop greeted them, just inside the door. He looked worried and Spaceman figured it wasn't the case; he was probably trying to figure out how the hell to lose fifty pounds before his next departmental physical. "Couple junkies found the stiff," he said, sounding bored as he indicated two spaced-out Hispanics huddled in the corner.

"And they called it in?" Spaceman asked skeptically, trying to suck his gut in.

"Not exactly. One of them was outside puking in the gutter when we drove by and spotted him."

"Where's the body?"

"Through there."

They followed his pointing finger into the back room, where another cop waited.

Spaceman stepped by him. It wasn't as bad as he'd feared

it would be. Apparently the junkie who'd tossed his cookies had a very weak stomach. This particular body was almost tidy.

She was fully dressed, in jeans and teeshirt, lying face down, with a halo of hair spread out on the filthy floor. Her hands were bound in the back, and she had been shot once in the head.

Spaceman just studied the scene for a moment, not saying anything.

Blue moved up next to him. "Oh, damn," he said suddenly, his voice sounding funny. "Damnit anyway."

Spaceman looked at him. "What?"

"I know her."

Now that was funny. The broad on the floor sure didn't look like the kind of woman Maguire would number among his acquaintances. She certainly wouldn't fit in at Trader Vic's or any of those fancy places Blue probably went whenever he could. Spaceman waited for an explanation.

Blue took a breath. "She came into the office the other day. When you were off. Said she was scared of the guy she was shacking up with. She was afraid he was going to kill her."

"How shrewd of her. And what did you do?"

He looked sick. "What could I do? Nothing had happened. She didn't even have a name on the guy. Just . . . Wolf or some damned thing. What could I do?" This time it was a real question.

"Not a thing, partner. Not a damned thing."

"Hell, I didn't even get an address." Blue knelt next to the body and stared at it. "I told her to move out. But she decided to wait until after the holidays. So Merry Christmas, Miss Wexler."

Spaceman knew from painful experience that there was nothing he could say that would make Blue feel one damned bit better, so he just kept quiet.

◻   ◻   ◻

Later, when the body had been tagged, bagged, and finally removed, they went back to the car. The sightseers were all gone. Blue sat behind the wheel silently.

Spaceman lit a cigarette and, after a moment, held it out toward the other man. Blue took it and sucked in smoke almost desperately. He handed it back immediately.

After a few seconds, Blue snorted. "Everyone is so damned corruptible," he said. "That ten seconds of nicotine will cost me at the gym."

"My partner the saint."

"Oh, sure," Blue said, starting the car. "I'm just fucking wonderful."

9

She was a screamer.

He could never tell ahead of time which ones would do a lot of screaming in bed and which ones would go about the whole thing with such silent, sometimes even grim, determination that he wondered why they bothered.

Hannah, no doubt about it, was an exceedingly vocal broad. She didn't look the part. With her wardrobe of expensive but conservative suits, sensible pumps, and perfectly styled hair—not to mention the ever-present string of dully lustrous pearls—Hannah looked like the perfect wife for a Republican state senator.

Which is exactly what she happened to be. And very good at it she was, too. Perfect. Except, of course, for the one afternoon every two weeks when she broke all the rules.

Toby poured himself another glass of the Roederer Cristal, then put the bottle back into the ice bucket. Nothing but the best for Mrs. Senator's afternoons of sin and sex. He wondered if anyone at all out in Orange County knew about Hannah and her paid lover.

He glanced impatiently at the closed bathroom door. How the hell long was she going to stay in there this week?

Then, irritated at himself, he gave a small shrug. What difference did it make? She was paying a flat rate for his time, and if it was her choice to spend a good part of that time in the can, so be it. Actually, he should be glad; every minute she was in there meant less time he'd have to spend in the sack.

He sat down in the deep-cushioned chair and wriggled his bare toes in the carpet. The hotel sure knew how to take care of its guests. He sometimes wondered if the so-polite staff ever got curious about Hannah's visits. Probably not. Discretion was undoubtedly part of their job training.

Toby sipped his drink carefully, savoring the luxurious quiet of the moment. He had a taste for and appreciation of the good things in life. The best things, in fact. Booze, clothes, surroundings. Unfortunately, it was not so easy anymore to keep his lifestyle up to the level he enjoyed. Toby blamed his current financial difficulties on the government. Frigging Reaganomics. Tight money made it harder for the broads to account for what they spent. Harder to explain to an irate husband that occasional two or three hundred dollars.

Blaming the national economy was easier and less troubling than blaming any decline in business on his age. Thirty-six now. Not young anymore, by most standards, and in Los Angeles not being young was considered almost a capital offense.

The next sip he took of the champagne was a little larger.

But hell, even in this city that so idolized youth, age wasn't the only thing that mattered. Toby Reardon had class and the kind of broad he attracted wanted that. A woman like Hannah, for example, wasn't just interested in buying some bedroom athlete who could come ten times an hour. She wanted a lover who knew the perfect wine to order from room service and who could make bed talk in at least passable French.

What it came right down to was that Toby Reardon offered more to his clients than just a well-practiced cock. He sold a sense of style, damnit, and that was something not many eighteen-year-old studs had.

Still, he was smart enough to realize that sooner or later

time was going to catch up with him. At this point, probably sooner. He sighed.

Luckily, before he could get any more deeply mired in gloom, the bathroom door opened and Hannah came out. She was still wearing her lacy slip, but the suit and flowered blouse were gone, along with the practical pumps and panty hose. "Sorry to be so long, Toby," she said, just like she said every time.

"Always worth waiting for," he said easily. Gazing up at her, he trailed the base of the crystal glass slowly back and forth across his bare chest, nipple to nipple. She watched as a believer might have watched the snake being charmed in India. Then he held the glass, lightly balanced, on his denim-clad crotch. The damned jeans were two sizes too small, but the suffering paid off. "Want some?" he offered.

Hannah caught her breath. She was in her early fifties. Not in bad shape for a woman her age, though. Which proved that a little surgical tuck here and there could work wonders. Toby sometimes actually found himself considering something along those lines.

But he always dismissed the idea quickly. Hell, he didn't look a day over twenty-five.

Hannah was now sitting on the edge of the vast bed. Waiting. Although she was the paying customer, she never made the first move. It was as if she needed to be seduced, taken.

Well, it was his job to oblige.

Toby drained the last of the cool champagne, licking the stray drops from his upper lip, then stood. He unsnapped and unzipped the expensive, uncomfortable French jeans and pushed them slowly down his legs. Under the jeans, he was naked.

Hannah watched his approach warily.

"Take the slip off, Hannah," he ordered in a low voice.

She shivered a little, but otherwise didn't move.

"Take it off, bitch, or I'll rip it off."

They had the routine down perfectly.

She began to pull the slip off. When the piece of silk and lace was almost over her head, Toby reached out and yanked until Hannah-the-Senator's-Wife was sitting there naked. Except for the damned pearls, of course. Toby, still standing directly in front of her, ran two fingers around her neck, caressing the surface of the pearls more than that of her warm, scented flesh. He wondered what the necklace would go for.

Her breathing grew fast and labored.

"You look to me like a broad just asking to be raped," Toby said, still whispering, still guiding his fingers along her skin. Technique was what made them glad to pay for his services. He always seemed to know exactly what it was a woman wanted from him, whether that meant roughness or tenderness; sex that was quick and clean, or screwing that was sweaty and dirty. Whatever they weren't getting at home, he supposed.

Hannah was watching him, her eyes made unnaturally bright by both passion and contact lenses.

"A little rape in the afternoon. Beats the hell out of tea with the ladies in Sacramento, right, baby?"

She made an unintelligible sound that was somewhere between a groan and a sob.

Toby smiled and leaned against her until they both fell back onto the bed.

10

Lars made still another recon through the hotel lobby. His eyes moved constantly, checking out the endless flow of people around the marble arches. Underneath the crystal chandeliers, everyone looked tanned and successful. Most of all, these people all looked like they belonged. It was a private club and there wasn't any room in it for the bastard son of a Cleveland barmaid.

Lars self-consciously smoothed the front of his blue knit shirt, the one with the alligator on it. This was what it seemed liked everyone had been wearing the last time he was in the country, but now it seemed, what the hell was that word, déclassé. The fact that he felt uncomfortable here made him angry. To hell with them, he thought. All it took to join their damned special fraternity was money, and pretty soon he'd be a member in good standing.

He'd been hanging out in the lobby of the Beverly Wilshire for almost two hours now, watching and trying to remain inconspicuous. So far, except for a redheaded actress he remembered from some old television sitcom, nobody looked familiar.

But, he reminded himself, it had been a long time. If three years had passed since he'd last seen Dev, it must be four at least since Tobias Reardon's path had crossed his. He and Reardon were friends, too, good friends, but it was different from the relationship he had with Dev. More edgy or something. Maybe the difference had to do with the fact that Devlin Conway had class; he'd been born with it. Reardon, on the other hand, was, like himself, a street fighter from way back. Though they liked each other, there was always a degree of mistrust between them. Born of deeply ingrained memories, it could not be overcome, even by genuine affection.

Despite the years, though, when Lars finally did spot Reardon, he recognized the other man right away.

It happened on El Camino Real, the private, cobblestone street that connected the two lobbies of the hotel. Lars was standing under one of the authentic gaslights, finishing a cigarette, when he saw Reardon coming toward him.

He was wearing tight jeans, a white V-neck sweater that had to be cashmere set off by a single thin gold chain around a very tanned neck, and shiny loafers with no socks. His brown hair was cut long and his eyes were hidden by large mirrored sunglasses.

Lars watched him move quickly but gracefully through the crowd. Amazing, but the damned gutter rat seemed to fit in very nicely. Still, there was something a little different in his carriage, maybe a slight tension to his spine that set him apart.

Lars waited until Reardon was past, then fell into step just behind him. "Hear you been screwing around with my wife," he said softly.

Toby stopped abruptly and his shorter form seemed to brace itself slightly. Then he moved again. "Fuck off," he muttered.

"You haven't changed a bit, you bastard."

He stopped again, turning this time so he could see who was speaking to him. After a moment, he grinned. "Shit. What rock did you crawl out from under?"

Lars shifted the heavy ashtray closer and then took a sip of the too-sweet drink he'd ordered in the hotel pub. They hadn't said much yet. Toby seemed to be waiting for him to make the first move. That was symptomatic of their relationship—neither man wanted to give an inch, risk handing the other an edge. Street kids playing king of the hill.

Lars smoked and drank for another minute or so, deciding just how best to play this scene. "You seem to be doing okay," he said finally.

Toby shrugged. "I get along."

Lars almost smiled. More games. Toby didn't want him to think he was a failure, but then again, just in case Morgan was leading up to a request for money, he didn't want to come off like he was rolling in the stuff. "Well, getting along is good," he said thoughtfully. "But would you be interested in doing much better?"

Toby drank with a kind of practiced ease; the practice showed. "Which means?"

"Which means making a lot of money."

"What's your definition of a lot of money?"

"A million dollars. Just for you."

A faint and sardonic smile flickered briefly beneath the disconcerting mirrors. "Okay. Who do I have to shtup?"

Lars smiled, too, and shook his head. "Nobody. You can keep your cock in your pants on this deal. And once it all comes down, you won't be fucking anybody unless you want to."

"I already do that. Mine is a very selective clientele."

Lars took another sip of the drink, beginning to get used to the sticky taste. Then he reached across the small table with one hand and lifted the damned Ray-Bans so that he could see the shrewd hazel eyes he knew were hidden there. "A few lines starting to show up, lover boy. Well, we're all getting older." He dropped the glasses back into place.

Toby frowned.

"Well?"

He looked around the room. "See that broad over there, Lars? The one in the grey suit?"

Lars looked. "I see her."

"She's married to one of the most powerful men in the state. That's an aide to the governor she's having a drink with now. But just a little while ago, she was upstairs being royally screwed by yours truly."

"God. She looks old enough to be your mother."

"No, not really. But the point is, I do my act for her and she hands me two hundred dollars. Plus, this time, a hundred-dollar Christmas bonus."

"I once saw a trained seal do his act for a couple of dried fish. At least your pay is better."

"Fuck you, Lars."

He grinned. "Hell, no, I can't afford you."

"That much money, man, for what amounts to jacking off. It's a simple life. No hassles, no danger, and all the free booze I can drink."

Lars shrugged, as if it didn't matter to him one way or the other. "Hey, Tobias, if you're happy, fine. I was only making the offer. I just thought it would be good to get the three of us together again."

"Three? You're saying that Devlin Conway is in on this?" Toby sounded surprised.

"Sure."

"Sure, he would be," Toby said softly. "You two were always tight." He frowned again, looking across the room at the broad. "Okay, Wolf, what's going on?"

The old nickname brought a smile to his face. He leaned across the table confidentially. "Remember our diamonds?" he said softly.

This time, Toby lowered the glasses himself and peered at Lars. "Sheee-it," he breathed, sounding, even after twenty-five years away, like the son of an Oklahoma dirt farmer.

11

Spaceman was halfway through his cheeseburger by the time Blue came into the restaurant. Although, in truth, "restaurant" was probably a rather glorified term for this particular eating establishment. Owned and operated single-handedly by Joe Spinoza, a retired cop, the food that was served up in the diner was most often praised with the word "filling." But it was right next to the cop shop, the prices were right, and Joe always had a kind word for his customers. There were days, many days, when a cop needed a friendly face more than haute cuisine.

As Blue entered, he shut the door with considerably more ferocity than the job required and came over to the counter.

Spaceman put the remains of the burger down and twisted on the stool to look at his partner. The blond settled next to him, carefully straightening the crease in his grey slacks, and folded his hands on the counter. Neither man spoke.

Joe pulled himself away from the soap opera on his omnipresent television and came over. "Hiya, Maguire. What can I get for you today?"

Blue pretended to study the grease-stained mimeographed menu that never changed. "Grilled cheese," he said at last. "And some skim milk."

"Comin' up." Joe turned half of his attention to the grill. The other half was split evenly between the unmarried, pregnant, drug-addict daughter of the town doctor on the soap and whatever Spaceman or Blue might say.

Spaceman maneuvered a french fry through the watery red pool of catsup on his plate. "So what's going on down at stiff city?" he asked.

Blue grimaced before giving the expected reply. "Kind of dead."

Spaceman grinned, not at the tired line, but at the fact that Blue had actually said it.

Joe, however, laughed out loud. He loved the cops who came in, delighted in their gruesome, stale jokes about the work they did. He was generous with the food and also with the advice he liked to dispense.

"Seriously," Spaceman said. "Did you see her?"

"Her?" Said with elaborate blandness.

"Sharon, of course."

"Oh. I saw her. She did the post."

Spaceman lifted his burger again, took a bite, chewed vigorously, swallowed impatiently. "When the hell are you going to tell me what's going on between you two?"

"Nothing's going on."

"Obviously. That's what I mean."

"There's nothing to tell." Blue poured the milk from its wax carton into the plastic tumbler and took a sip. "Maybe we should talk business. If I need any help with my love life, I'll write Dear Abby."

"If you'd rather," Spaceman said somewhat huffily.

"I'd much rather." Blue contemplated the television for a moment, watching Cathy Rigby McCoy talk perkily about sanitary napkins. "Something occurred to me a little while ago."

Spaceman, almost despite himself, had developed a certain respect for Maguire's mind during their partnership. The man not only had a master's degree, but he also had the smarts not to let that fact keep him from thinking. "What occurred to you?" Spaceman asked around the last bite of cheeseburger.

"About the Hua killing and Marybeth Wexler."

"Yeah, so?"

"Both of them were shot once in the back of the head."

"Believe it or not," Spaceman said with an edge, "I had noticed that myself."

Joe set a plate in front of Blue. "Execution style, is that what you're saying?"

"Ms. Patrolperson of the Year already pointed that out," Spaceman said.

Blue unfolded the paper napkin. "I'm not saying much of anything yet. Except that maybe we've been so busy thinking about Marybeth's damned roommate that we've missed the big picture."

"Ah, the big picture," Spaceman said. He slid open the plastic door on the dessert case and took out the last piece of day-old, supermarket apple pie.

Joe was getting interested now, leaving the knocked-up druggie to fend for herself. "You're thinking mob, right? Now there's a theory I could really get my teeth into and run with."

"Why don't we run it up the flagpole and see who salutes?" Spaceman said with a grin.

Blue was concentrating very hard on the charred sandwich. "I'm glad you're so amused by murder," he muttered.

Spaceman felt a little guilty; there wasn't much sport involved in bringing down a wounded animal. Blue, he realized, was really bothered by the Wexler broad's death, seeming to feel some sense of responsibility for the murder. That guilt, added to a certain feeling of uncertainty about his own abilities as a detective, made Maguire easy prey. "Murder isn't funny," Spaceman said.

"Just my theories about it, right?"

"What're you bellyaching about, Blue? Just tell me what the hell it is you're thinking. Who would be interested in executing a gook restaurant owner and a cheap tramp like, uh, Wexler?"

"I don't know who. Or why." He reached inside his

pocket and pulled out an envelope. "But I just picked up the ballistics reports on both killings."

Spaceman gave him a dirty look. "You couldn't have just said that in the beginning?"

"And ruin the suspense?" Now Blue grinned as he dropped the envelope onto the counter. "Anybody like to make a stab at what these reports say?"

Spaceman sighed. "Let me. Wexler and Hua were offed by the same goddamned gun."

"That's very possible. Both of them were taken out with nine-millimeter ammo. The bullets might have come from the same weapon. Maybe a Browning or a Luger. Could be a Walther. You figured that out nicely. Anybody ever tell you that you'd make a great detective, Kowalski?"

"Not lately." Spaceman took a bite of the pie and chewed the sticky cardboard glumly.

Hell, things kept getting worse and worse, and he hadn't even started his Christmas shopping yet.

Blue spent the evening addressing Christmas cards. As he worked on those, he also worked on a special bottle of Caussade Armagnac. Behind him, the television flickered on silently with some ridiculous holiday special. Noise was provided by the usual drone of the scanner.

Blue was startled when, soon after ten, the phone rang shrilly. He carefully licked one more envelope, sealed it, and then reached to answer. "Hello?"

"Hiya, Blue, it's just me again."

The funny thing was, Blue felt no sense of surprise at all. It was almost as if he'd just been killing time with the damned cards and the Armagnac, waiting for the call. "Who is this?" he asked, but the question was strangely passive, without any heat or even the real expectation of a response.

And, sure enough, there was no answer. Instead, the voice said, "I was just sitting here thinking about the old days. Do you ever think about those days, Loot?"

Blue lifted the crystal snifter and took a careful sip of the warm, light Armagnac. "I don't know what the hell you're talking about."

"Selective amnesia is what they call that, good buddy."

"I'm not being selective and I didn't say I've forgotten anything. I just don't understand, is all."

"Who does? I mean, who the hell does? Besides, all that stuff about the old days is boring, right? The past is so fucking boring."

There was a long stretch of silence across the wire. He inhaled the faint aroma of wood and earth and truffles held captive within the snifter. He was about ready to hang up.

"Man, it is snowing like hell out there."

Snow. Blue seized on that. "Out where?"

"In my frigging backyard, of course." The voice laughed, then sobered as suddenly. "Christ, we could have used some of this snow back then, right, Loot? It was so damned hot. You must remember how hot it was."

"Yeah . . . " Blue pressed the glass against his forehead.

"You want to know what I think?"

He didn't want to know. Definitely not. But he heard himself say, "What?"

"Sometimes I think that we all died in that place. We all died, but somebody fucked up and forgot to tell us. So now we're just fucking ghosts walking around, pretending to be alive. You ever feel like that, Loot?"

Blue shook his head.

Then he hung up.

He poured some more Armagnac and drank it, watching his hand shake.

12

Lars took another long pull on the bottle. This was good beer, Aass Bok, and he was enjoying it. In fact, he was enjoying the whole evening. It wasn't often he got the chance just to relax and be like other people. But with his feet propped on the railing of the small, trim boat named the *Homeport*, he could gaze out over Marina del Rey and think about the good life.

Toby emerged from the cabin with two more beers and a couple of sandwiches. He set the bottles and the plate down before sitting again.

"I had no idea there was so much money in sex," Lars said, indicating the surroundings with a lazy wave. "Maybe I would've become a lover instead of a fighter."

Toby grimaced. "The bank owns more of this thing than I do. But someday . . ."

"Someday soon."

"Maybe." Toby picked up one of the sandwiches and took a bite. He chewed thoughtfully for a moment.

"Of course, with the kind of money we're talking about here, buddy, you can get a boat that will make this one look like a garbage scow."

"I like this boat fine," Toby said mildly. He leaned back in the canvas deck chair and stared at Lars. The sunglasses had been discarded finally, replaced by horn-rims that his rich female clients probably never saw. They made him look rather like an intense grad student. "I might be interested in this, Lars. Maybe. But I want the bullshit to stop. Probably Devlin Conway will fall for whatever line of fast talk you lay on him, but he always was a sucker for you. I want the straight dope and I want it now."

Lars smiled. This was what he liked best about Toby; there was a minimum of crap to go through, once they quit sparring around. "Okay." He paused to watch a couple of women in shorts walk by on the dock. "I've been in touch with some connections in the local Vietnamese community. They tell me that the diamonds—our diamonds—are being brought into this country very soon. In fact, they might already be here, though I hope not."

"So who has them?"

"Names I don't know yet. But let's just say for the moment that the men in charge are mostly ex-officials from Saigon."

"That's a charming bunch to start messing with."

"Oh, it gets better." Lars picked up the other sandwich and looked at it. Thick slices of ham and a pale brown mustard on sourdough bread.

"I'll just bet it gets better." Toby shook his head. "Well, give it all to me. What's supposed to happen to the diamonds once they get here?"

"Now that's where things start to turn just a little sticky," Lars mumbled around a large bite.

"I can imagine."

He swallowed. "You remember those government guys from the old days. Always some kind of deal coming down. I don't have all the details yet, but rumor has it that the diamonds are to be exchanged for certain territorial concessions."

Toby made a gesture of irritation. "What the hell does that mean? Talk English, why don't you?"

"Specifically, the diamonds are being used to secure the right to distribute products of a pharmaceutical nature within a certain territory."

Toby tossed a bread crust to an impatiently waiting gull.

"Drugs and two-bit hoods. Wonderful. Didn't I just see this in a movie? You know, Lars, that kind of individual will kill you before breakfast and not even think about it."

"There are risks, I admit."

"Oh, you admit it. That makes me feel much better." Toby looked at him, then shook his head slowly. "Maybe you've just spent too long in the damned jungle. Your perspective on real life is truly warped."

Lars gave him a chilly glance. "Hey, babe, this is just an invitation, not an order. I'm not your frigging commanding officer anymore. You can tell me to take off and I'll be gone."

"How much of this did you lay on Conway?"

"None, really. I like to operate on the old need-to-know basis."

"And he still agreed to sign on?"

"Yes, of course."

"Of course." Toby stood. He walked to the bow and stared off into the distance.

Lars, knowing that a good salesman never pushes the smart customer too hard, kept quiet, finishing the beer and sandwich.

Finally Toby turned around. "Okay," he said quietly. "I'm in."

"Good."

Toby seemed to be waiting for Lars to say something more, but when he didn't, Reardon just turned back and leaned on the railing again.

Lars smiled to himself, turning the empty beer bottle in his fingers absently.

13

Somebody was ringing the doorbell, pressing a persistent finger on the button, and whoever it was seemed quite willing to keep it up until there was a response from inside.

Stubborn bastard.

Blue was only about half awake, his mind still fuzzed with liquor and the lingering fragments of a bad dream. He swore under his breath as he rolled off the couch. Nobody ever just dropped by his place. Except, occasionally, Spaceman Kowalski. The thought of trying to deal with his partner in this condition was intimidating.

But when he finally managed to reach the foyer, unlock, and open the door, it wasn't Spaceman he found there. Still, there was something familiar about the slouched figure in the baseball cap and windbreaker.

For one befuddled and almost terrifying moment, Blue thought that the phantom voice on his telephone had taken shape on the front porch. Then he relaxed, feeling foolish, as the face beneath the cap came into clear focus. It was a face that he had seen only in photographs, but he recognized the boy.

"You're Robbie Kowalski," he said.

"Yeah. I'm looking for Detective Blue Maguire."

"Well, you just found him."

The kid looked skeptical. He studied Blue, his eerily familiar gaze skimming over the Mexican wedding shirt and wrinkled white pants above bare feet. Blue reached up to try and straighten his hair, realizing belatedly that an empty brandy snifter still dangled from his hand. "You're my dad's partner?" Robbie finally said.

"I am, yes."

"Shit."

Blue wanted to explain that these were not his working clothes. That he didn't usually run around without shoes. That . . . . Instead, he just stepped to one side. "Come on in." It was his house, after all, and he could damned well run around it any way he wanted to. Unexpected visitors would just have to take him as he was. And this visitor was certainly unexpected. An unpleasant thought struck him suddenly. "He's okay? I mean, nothing's happened to Spaceman?"

Robbie shrugged. "Not as far as I know. He went out to Azusa or someplace. To get laid, I think."

Sweet kid.

"So what can I do for you?"

"To start with, you could gimme a beer."

"You're underage."

Robbie shot him a look.

Blue sighed. "Okay," he said. "One."

They walked into the kitchen. While Robbie took a bottle from the fridge, Blue dropped a level teaspoon of instant coffee into a heavy mug. After a moment's deliberation, he added another spoonful. Time to sober up. He then filled the mug with water from the automatic boiling tap and stirred. Put in some sugar for energy, but skipped the cream.

They went back into the living room, with Robbie already working on the beer. "What time is it, anyway?" Blue asked.

" 'Bout twelve."

"Damn." Another evening had somehow slipped away. "Shouldn't you be home in bed?"

"As far as anybody else knows, I am."

"I see." Blue waited, hoping for a sudden jolt of energy from the strong coffee. When it didn't come, he sighed again and took a closer look at the intruder. "I doubt that you came all the way up here from your mother's place just to cadge a beer. And speaking of which, how did you get here from Santa Monica?

"Hitched, of course."

Of course. "Not smart. There are a lot of crazies out there." He felt, suddenly, pretty sober. Maybe it was the coffee, or maybe it was the memory of one crazy in particular, Tom Hitchcock, who killed boys not so different from Robbie and who also came very close to killing a cop named Blue Maguire.

"Life is full of risks," Robbie said, seemingly unconcerned. He had already drained the beer. "One more, hey? It's frigging Christmas almost."

"All right. But that's it."

When Robbie was sitting again, they drank in silence for a few minutes. Blue half listened to a robbery-in-progress call on the scanner.

"You and my old man," Robbie said finally. "You're pretty tight, huh?"

"I guess." Blue thought about it. "Yeah, we're friends."

"Why?"

He sipped at the dregs of the cooling coffee. "Why?"

"He's impossible."

Blue almost smiled. "Sometimes, yes."

"But you like him anyway."

"Yes." He finished the coffee and set the cup aside. "He saved my life, you know."

"For real?"

"For very real." Blue poked at the top of his mouth with his tongue; the damned coffee had burned him and now it would be sore for days. He was also stalling, because he didn't want to talk about the whole thing with Hitchcock and his brother, or about the dead boys. Or especially about his own kidnapping. But he started and went through the whole sordid, sad mess. It sounded like a made-for-TV movie. A Spelling/Goldberg production.

When he finally was finished, one part of him wanted to reach out for the damned bottle and pour himself a healthy shot, but he didn't.

Robbie shrugged. "Well, I guess you'd almost have to like somebody who saved your ass like that."

Irritated that the boy seemed to have missed the point, Blue shook his head. "That's not it. I mean, what happened, happened. We're partners, so he was only doing what was right." God, how pompous he sounded. "That doesn't explain or define our relationship." Blue was aware that he was falling into an old and dangerous trap—talking like a textbook on human psychology instead of a real person.

"So, my old man's a big-deal cop. Heavily into running around with his macho gun and saving people."

"Don't make some kind of mockery out of it," Blue said sharply. "You have no right to do that."

"I have no right," Robbie repeated slowly. "Bullshit." He drank deeply, then lowered the can and glared at Blue. "I do have the fucking right, Mr. Cop. And I also have a question."

"Ask."

"If the great and wonderful Spaceman Kowalski is so into saving people, why the hell didn't he save me?"

Blue didn't know what question he had been expecting, but this certainly wasn't it. "What?"

Robbie seemed totally unaware of the tears that were suddenly standing in his eyes. "I was out there all alone and I was scared, Maguire. That's why I kept setting those fires in the hills. If I could've burned down the whole fucking county I would have, because I wanted him to find me and stop me. To save me. He saved you and all those other people, so why couldn't he save me? I'm his son." The last words were said in a hoarse whisper.

"He tried, Robbie."

"Oh, sure, he tried." Disgust dripped from the voice.

"I was there, boy. I saw him going through hell because you were missing. But the point is, he had those other boys to think about, too. And then me. He just kept pushing himself to do it all."

"But the real point is, partner, the goddamned point is, he didn't save me. He just didn't." Robbie shrugged. "How'd you get him to like you?"

Again, Blue was puzzled. "What?"

"I want my father to like me."

"Robbie, he loves you." Blue almost said more; he wanted to grab the boy and shake the knowledge into him of how lucky he was to have a father who did care so much.

An expression that tried to be a sneer crossed Robbie's face. It failed, however, and resolved itself into anguish. "I know he loves me. That's his job. But I want him to like me, too. I want him to be my friend, like he's your friend."

Blue felt absolutely helpless. "Maybe," he said carefully, "it can't be that way. A father is one thing and a friend is something else." He poked at the burned spot again, hoping pain might be inspirational. "I had an old man who really didn't care about me," he said after a moment. "That's much worse. Maybe getting Spaceman Kowalski for a friend now is my reward for that." He smiled faintly. "Or my punishment. Sometimes I'm not sure."

Robbie snorted. "Okay. Well, I'm sorry I bothered you." He stood, crushing the beer can in one hand. "I'll just take off."

"Hold on, kiddo. I'm not sending you off into the night to hitch your way back to Santa Monica. Let me put some shoes on and I'll drive you."

"Don't bother."

"Hey, all I need to do is let something happen to you. I don't need Spaceman Kowalski on my case, thank you very much."

"But you two are such good buddies, right?" All the earlier vulnerability was gone from Robbie's voice now. He was just being a smartass kid.

"No sense pressing my luck," Blue replied. He smiled.

After a moment, Robbie smiled back at him.

14

Spaceman lost the daily toss of the coin and so he was driving again. Usually he didn't mind that chore and even enjoyed the feel of the expensive car in his hands. But not on a day that included still more rain and the holiday crowds. The festive decorations in the city were starting to look distinctly soggy.

He stretched as best he could behind the wheel. "I feel like my joints are starting to rust," he bitched.

"Uh-huh." Blue was watching the clogged traffic listlessly.

Spaceman was beginning to feel like he'd had more company back in the days when he worked alone than he did now. "You okay?"

"What?" Blue glanced at him, seeming to consider something. "I've been getting these phone calls," he said finally.

"What kind of calls?"

He shrugged. "Anonymous ones."

"Dirty?"

"Not so's I could notice." They smiled. "No, this is different. Somebody I know. Should know. I think probably somebody I was in Nam with."

"So what's going on? Threats?"

Blue shook his head, then waved a disparaging hand. "Hell, it's probably nothing. Forget I even said anything."

"Okay," Spaceman said agreeably. "It's absolutely forgotten."

They both knew that it wasn't, of course.

The address they were looking for on Crenshaw turned out to belong to a ramshackle wooden house that was the headquarters of something called the Los Angeles Vietnamese Center. Since the trail on Marybeth Wexler was leading them nowhere very fast, they were trying to track down what they could on Hua.

A small group of teenage boys was gathered on the porch, out of the rain, smoking and listening to rock music on a massive ghetto blaster. Spaceman and Blue got out of the car and dodged raindrops all the way to the porch. Once under cover of the eaves, they stopped, looking at the boys.

The boys looked back. "Cops," a voice said.

"Hey, Mr. Policeman, we haven't broken any laws."

"Glad to hear it," Spaceman said. "Even if I don't believe it. Unfortunately, we don't have time to waste on small-fry like you guys today. We're looking for whoever's in charge here."

"Sorry," the first boy said. "We don't speak any English." The words were said almost completely without accent.

Blue opened the door, held it for Spaceman, then followed him through.

"Asshole kids," Spaceman muttered. "Not even over here long enough to get the rice out of their ears and already they've turned into creeps just like the natives."

Blue resisted the urge to smile.

The living room of the old house had been turned into a reception area. Posters and flyers covered most of the peeling wallpaper. The room was dominated by a large desk, which was in turn occupied by a beautiful young woman. At the moment, she was bent over an ancient Underwood, typing swiftly.

Spaceman stayed by the door, letting Blue move in to do the talking. It was strictly a judgment call, this daily division of labor, and from the first, they had generally called it right.

She let him stand there for a full minute, before deigning to look up. "Yes?"

He held up his ID perfunctorily. "I'm Detective Maguire, L.A.P.D."

She studied the badge and picture too long. At last, she raised her eyes to him.

Blue, well aware of the game she was playing, flipped the wallet closed and put it away. "Do you know a man named Don Hua?"

She glanced at Spaceman, who was reading the posters on the wall, then back at Blue. "That question should be phrased in the past tense, shouldn't it?"

"Yes, I suppose so. That means you did know him?"

"I knew of him. We are not so large a community and my position here brings me into contact with most of our people living in this area."

"So did it ever bring you into contact with Hua?"

She lifted a slender hand. "I cannot say yes or no for certain."

"We're trying to find out who murdered him."

"And, of course, I wish you luck in that endeavor."

"Do you have any ideas at all to offer, Miss—?"

"Tran. Angel Tran. Ideas?"

"About who might have wanted Hua dead?"

She pretended to think. "No. But there are a great many Americans who do not like us. Who hate us, in fact. Perhaps because we are a reminder of an unhappy time."

"Are you saying that you think Hua was killed by an American?"

She smiled. "Without being ethnocentric, I feel that, statistically, the chances are excellent."

"Touché."

"Perhaps one of your former soldiers."

Blue put both hands into his pants pockets and rocked back and forth for a moment. "I'm a former soldier, as it happens."

"Then you are surely not ignorant of the hostility so many of your fellows feel for us."

Spaceman spoke for the first time. "Maybe they feel that there's something to be bitter about." He was still staring at the wall.

Blue glanced over at him, then shook his head. "Miss Tran, perhaps the emotions are misplaced, but I'm sure you can understand them."

She said nothing.

"What about Hua?"

"There's nothing I can tell you."

Spaceman turned around. "Did you know a woman named Marybeth Wexler?"

"No."

"Maybe Hua knew her."

"I cannot say, of course."

"Of course." Blue put one of his cards on the edge of her desk. "If you hear of anything that might concern this case, you'll call, Miss Tran?"

"Of course. Isn't that what any law-abiding person would do?"

He nodded.

As they left, she started typing again.

The boys were still on the porch. They looked very settled in, as if it were a frequent resting place. "Some car, cop," one said. "Graft must be up this year."

Blue just smiled.

When they were back in the Porsche again, he stared out the window thoughtfully at the boys. "I saw your kid last night," he said abruptly.

"Robbie?"

"You have another one you've been hiding? Yes, Robbie."

"Where'd you see him?"

"He came by my place."

"Why the hell?"

"Mostly just to meet me, I think."

Spaceman started the car, gunning the engine. "Well, I'm sure that must have been a real thrill for all concerned."

Blue recognized the tone in his partner's voice and he was smart enough to shut up.

15

Devlin Conway took two steps backward and surveyed the wall of photographs critically. He had been at this for over three hours now, arranging and rearranging the display. Addison had given up in disgust finally and taken the bimbo to dinner, leaving one very nervous photographer alone. Which suited him just fine.

He perched on the edge of the desk to light a cigarette, hoping that a shot of nicotine would soothe his jangled nerves. More than just the upcoming show was bothering him and he knew what it was. He couldn't stand this hanging around in one place so long, being totally consumed with the past. With pictures of a time and place that almost seemed to belong to another man's memory. It was all beginning to rub against him. His hands itched to hold a camera again. As it was now, he felt like the unwilling subject of his own lens, a figure frozen in time and space.

There was soft, unexpected knock on the door that startled him. Addison wasn't supposed to be back; he'd given Devlin the key with which to lock up. Devlin hesitated, then went to peer out into the gathering night. When he recognized who was standing there, he paused for another beat, before unlocking and opening the door.

Lars charged in. "How's it going?" he asked breezily.

"All right. Considering. I was wondering when you'd show up. Or even if."

He looked offended. "I told you, didn't I?"

"You told me."

"So have a little faith, mate," Lars chided. He saw his picture hanging on the wall, frowned a little, then moved slowly around the room, looking at the other photos. "This is good shit, you know."

"I know. I'm a damned good photographer."

They grinned at one another.

"So what about it, Lars? What's happening?"

"Big things, big things. Tobias is in. It's starting to move. Like a damned snowball rolling downhill."

Devlin wished that Lars could somehow manage to sound less like a carnival barker promoting the glories of the freak show. "And what am I supposed to do? Besides try to stay out of the avalanche?"

"Nothing for the moment."

"That sounds too easy."

Lars, still looking at the pictures, stretched and rubbed the back of his neck. "When I need you, you'll be available. To cover my back. That's what matters."

"And just for that, I get a rather large fortune."

"Sure." Lars walked over to him. "Don't worry about it."

"Right." Devlin began to stack some papers on the desk. "Let me ask you a question. And I'd like a straight answer, please."

Lars looked injured. "I always give you straight answers."

"Maybe I just don't ask the right questions then."

"Maybe. So what's this question?"

"Just how dangerous is this thing we're into?"

"Oh, pretty dangerous."

"You seem to take that fact rather lightly."

Lars smiled. "People have been shooting at me for a very long time. Nobody's hit me yet."

Devlin cast him a skeptical look. "Ha. I remember differently."

Lars rubbed his left side ruefully. "Well, not fatally, at least. Not yet."

"Funny man."

He shrugged and seemed to dismiss the subject. "You know, Dev, come to think of it, I do have an errand to run later. Maybe you'd like to come along."

Although he spoke offhandedly, Devlin got the idea that this was the true purpose of his visit. "To cover your ass, right?"

"Oh, maybe. But mostly just for the fun of it. I don't expect any flak tonight. Just some conversation."

Devlin considered his options, then nodded. "All right. I've done all the damage I can here for right now anyway."

"Great," Lars said, obviously pleased. "We'll go grab some chow first. It'll be just like old times, buddy."

That, in Devlin's view at least, was a tempered joy, but as usual, he was caught up by the other man's enthusiasm. He turned off the lights and paused only long enough to lock the door as he followed Lars out.

16

It had been a long day, and not until the very end of it did Blue point out that they hadn't yet searched Hua's apartment, which was being kept under police seal, pending just such a visit. Spaceman was ready to quit for the night, past ready, but he tossed the file aside and stood. "We might as well get that out of the way," he said wearily.

Blue nodded agreement, just managing to catch the keys that Spaceman pitched toward him suddenly.

"You drive."

Hua had lived alone in an apartment not far from his restaurant. They got a key from the Hispanic manager, who explained in rapid-fire Spanish that he had no idea who might have wanted to kill that poor bastard Hua, it was very, very tragic, and when would he be able to rent the apartment again, because he was losing money every day, and as a poor refugee (poor, but legal, he added quickly) trying to make his way in this wonderful country, he needed every cent.

Blue didn't bother translating all of that to Spaceman, who was lost after the first ten words spewed out. "We'll be done as quickly as possible," he said in much slower, but excellent, Spanish. "Then it's yours."

The man bowed and expressed his undying gratitude.

"You know what I think," Spaceman said as they climbed the stairs to 2B.

"What's that?"

"I think that pretty soon there aren't going to be any real, English-speaking Americans left in this city at all."

"Like us, you mean?"

"Damned right, like us."

"Well," Blue said, removing the police seal and unlocking the door, "you may be right."

"Count on it," Spaceman said glumly.

"Then maybe you better brush up on your Spanish. Just in case I'm not around to interpret."

"You better be around. But, anyway, fuck 'em if they can't speak the right language." They stepped into the apartment. "Shit."

The room was very clean and almost empty. A few straw mats on the linoleum floor and a small statue of Buddha in one corner were the only furnishings, other than a small television and a low, black lacquer table.

"Mr. Hua was evidently a man of simple tastes," Blue said.

"I guess. Hell, it looks like a monk or something lived here." Spaceman walked over to another door and pushed it open. The bedroom, apparently. More mats, a dresser, and an old desk. "He must've slept on the damned floor."

"Quite an ascetic."

"Quite a nut," Spaceman muttered. He sat down in front of the desk and opened a drawer.

Blue started on the dresser. It didn't take him long to go through the meager supply of clean, if threadbare, under- wear and socks.

"According to these papers," Spaceman said, "Hua was some kind of minor big shot in Saigon."

Blue finished with the dresser and went to the closet. "That was one thing there was never a shortage of over there. Minor big shots."

"True. Most of this I can't understand." Spaceman looked

up. "I don't suppose that reading Vietnamese is among your many talents?"

"Unfortunately not. I could toss off a few choice obscenities from the guards in the Hanoi Hilton, but they probably wouldn't help much." His voice was muffled, coming from the back of the closet. "This looks interesting."

"What?"

Blue emerged, holding a small wooden box in both hands. "It was on the shelf, behind some books." He brought the box to the desk and set it down.

Spaceman raised the lid, then gave a soft whistle. "Nice piece."

Blue lifted the shiny, French-made pistol carefully and checked it. "Loaded, too." He sniffed the barrel. "Hasn't been fired lately."

While Blue unloaded the gun, Spaceman searched through the other things in the box. "More papers. Some military insignia. Immigration documents. And this." He held up a snapshot, holding it between two fingers.

The picture showed a younger Hua and an American Marine grinning into the camera. They were flanking a third man who wore the black pajamas of the Viet Cong. The third man wasn't smiling, because he was quite dead. Hua was holding a pistol that looked like the one they'd just found, while the American made a V-for-victory sign. Or maybe it was V-for-peace.

The photo made Blue feel a little sick. Still, he took it from Spaceman for a closer look. The American was slender and fair-haired, with a grin that went no further than his lips. His eyes, seemingly untouched by humor or any other emotion, stared not really at the camera itself, but at the invisible photographer. Blue turned the picture over and studied the Viet writing on the back. "We'll have to find somebody to translate this."

"I guess. A waste of time, probably."

"Maybe. But I'd be interested in knowing more about this guy here."

Spaceman took the picture back and stared at the face. "Hell, I'd lay odds that anybody as whacked out as that turkey never made it back to the world."

Blue shrugged. "We'll see."

"But not tonight, my boy. As Scarlett O'Hara said, tomorrow is another day. Let's get all this shit packed up and get the hell out of here."

Blue nodded, still studying the face in the picture as Spaceman started gathering the papers.

17

Lars parked around the corner from the building on Olympic. He reached for a Gitane and then offered the pack to Devlin, who took one as well.

"Just what are we about to do here?" Devlin asked after two puffs.

"Nothing much. Just talk."

"To whom?"

"If my dope is the straight stuff, to Phillipe Tran."

"Phillipe?" Devlin thought back. "The general's son, right? He's in this country?"

Lars pointed at a black notebook on the backseat. "The book never lies." He opened the car door. "Time to start earning your cut, Mr. Conway," he said with a grin.

Devlin, still not quite sure about this, hesitated, then got out of the car and followed him.

The ground floor of the building they approached housed a fresh vegetable and fruit store, which was closed up for the night by now. They walked past the store entrance, to a side door. A quick check of the mailboxes in the cramped entrance hall netted them one with the name Tran scribbled on it in magic marker. "Bingo," Lars said with satisfaction.

They climbed one flight and he knocked softly on the door of apartment B. Devlin stood just behind him, off a little to one side. He wondered for the first time if maybe he shouldn't have a gun or something. It was a thought that startled him. Was Lars armed? No doubt; Devlin didn't think that he'd ever seen the other man without a gun. Usually more than one. Whether that fact should have reassured or frightened him, he didn't know.

After a minute, a young man opened the door. He wore jeans and a teeshirt and held a can of Coke in one hand. "Yeah? What you want?"

"You Phillipe Tran?"

"Maybe. Maybe not. Who wants to know?"

"We do."

"Yeah? So?"

"Don't you remember us? We were friends of your father, in Saigon." Lars leaned against the wall.

"Saigon? I don't remember nothing about Saigon."

"Sure you can."

He lifted the can for a quick gulp. "I didn't say I can't remember. I just don't."

Devlin moved forward a little. "You can certainly remember us, Phillipe. We spent a lot of time at your family's home."

"Yeah. You're the photographer." He glanced at Lars. "And you're Wolf. I knew it the minute I opened the door."

"Good boy," Lars said.

"I remember that you're the ones who were going to help make my father a rich man and then bring us all to America. Instead, he got dead and my mother, sister, and I were forgotten."

Lars tapped the wall impatiently with his hand. "It was your old man who came to us with the plan," he said. "Not the other way around."

Tran shrugged.

"Anyway, you made it here after all, right?"

"Oh, yes, sure. We came on a boat with two hundred people stuffed into a space made for half that number. My mother died on the trip and they threw her body into the water as breakfast for the fish."

"I'm sorry," Devlin said.

Tran glanced at him. "Why? Did you kill my father?"

"No, of course not."

"Well, then?"

Devlin shook his head helplessly.

Lars sighed. "Look, enough old times. We're here to talk about the diamonds."

"Diamonds?" Tran smiled. "Do I look like a man who has diamonds? I work in the market downstairs."

"You don't have the rocks, but I think you might know something about them."

"Not me. All I know about is peddling vegetables. Sorry."

Before either of the other two knew what was happening, Lars reached out with one hand to grab Tran around the neck, lifting and pinning him against the door. The smaller man's feet dangled off the floor.

Devlin, startled, took two steps backward. Damn, he thought, I should have my bloody camera. The harsh back-lighting from the apartment, the palatable violence, the tab-leau of the two men against the unpainted wooden door would make a great shot.

"Now listen up, you gook bastard. You know me. You know I mean business, right?"

Lars' voice jolted Devlin back to the moment. The words were said in a tone he hadn't heard in a long time.

Tran, gasping, managed to nod.

"Because we're such old friends, I'm going to give you a little time to think this over. But when we come back, you better be ready to talk. You get what I'm saying?"

Another nod.

"Terrific." Lars suddenly released his hold and Tran nearly fell to the floor in a heap. He caught himself, just managing to stay on his feet. "Come on, Dev," Lars said. He walked away without looking back.

After a moment, Devlin followed.

18

Spaceman was glad and more than a little surprised to see that the garage had actually delivered his car as promised. Instead of getting behind the wheel of the clunker right after leaving the office, though, he walked across the street to the Lock-up. Skirting the other just-off-duty cops, a group which did not include his partner, he sat alone at the far end of the bar.

He thought his way through a bottle of beer.

When the last of the Coors was gone, instead of ordering another and settling in for the evening, Spaceman slid from the barstool and went to the phone in the corner. After his coins had been deposited, he was treated to a cacophony of strange clankings and clunkings along the line. It seemed to him that things had gone downhill with telephones ever since the frigging breakup of good old Ma Bell. That lady might have been a bitch who delighted in holding the ordinary slob over a barrel, but at least she knew how to run a phone company. Spaceman had very little faith in amateurs.

It was his hope that Robbie would answer the call, but no such luck. "Yes?" came the crisp voice.

The woman could never say hello like everybody else. "Karen? It's me."

"What?"

"Well, merry Christmas to you, too."

She sighed. "Sorry, but it's been a very long day."

"Yeah, well, tell me about it." He paused, reading the various obscenities scrawled on the wall next to the phone. If you stopped to consider that almost all the patrons of this place were either cops or lawyers, with an occasional judge thrown in for good measure, the blatant and mostly perverted messages might be considered a little scary. "Robbie there?"

"Yes, why?" she said suspiciously.

"Because I'm coming out to see him."

"What's the matter?" Now she sounded a little scared.

If she didn't aggravate him so damned much, he might have felt sorry for her. "Nothing's the matter, for Chrissake, I just want to talk to him. Is there something wrong with that?"

Although he was sure that she would have loved to come up with something, apparently nothing came to mind, so she just told him to drive on out if he wanted to, and hung up.

Spaceman went back to toss some money onto the bar and left.

So far, the meeting between father and son hadn't been a smashing success. It just seemed to be following the same old pattern. Robbie came out of the house when Spaceman sounded the horn and joined him in the car. They exchanged polite greetings and at that point, conversation lagged.

Finally, out of desperation and also because he hadn't had any dinner and was hungry, Spaceman drove to the nearby McDonald's, and they went inside. Now, with cheeseburgers, fries, and Cokes on the table between them, he was determined to get said whatever it was that had to be said. Even if he still didn't know what the hell that was.

"I hear you paid a visit to my partner last night," he said, sprinkling too much salt on his fries.

"Yeah, the famous Blue Maguire. What the hell kind of name is that, anyway?"

Spaceman shrugged. "He once told me that his father named him after an old hunting dog."

"You believe that?"

"Maybe."

Robbie put extra catsup on his cheeseburger. "A genuine creep."

"You think so?" Spaceman said mildly. "That's funny, most people sort of like him."

The boy seemed a little embarrassed. "He was okay, I guess. Just not what I was expecting. You two don't seem real, what's the word, compatible."

"We're not planning on getting married. Blue is okay. A good partner."

"Well, terrific," Robbie said with unexpected sharpness.

Spaceman ate some cheeseburger. "Why'd you go to his place?"

Robbie shrugged. "He probably gave you a blow-by-blow account of the whole thing, so why ask me?"

"All he told me was that you were there. Nothing else."

A light flickered in the brown eyes. "Really? Maguire is a man with honor. Hell, better still, a cop with honor."

Spaceman just waited.

Robbie pulled the plastic lid from his Coke and took a gulp. He chewed on small pieces of ice for a moment. "I guess mostly I went there because I wanted to see what kind of guy he is. Because I know he's your friend and I wanted to understand why."

Spaceman took the last bite of the cheeseburger into his mouth. It gave him time to think as he chewed and swallowed. "What's to understand?"

"I don't know. Just why this one person is your friend. I don't know." Robbie began to gather the trash from the table and shove it into a sack. "You want it straight? I went to Maguire to see if he could tell me how to get you to like me. To be my friend. Dumb, huh?"

"I see," Spaceman said, although he wasn't sure he saw at all.

Robbie crushed the paper cup. "Can we split? I mean, Big Macs and heavy conversation don't exactly mix."

Spaceman nodded. As they left, he noticed a table in the corner was crowded with kids who seemed to know Robbie. His son walked out quickly, though, without glancing that way. Maybe their presence was the real reason he was in such a hurry to leave.

They drove back to the house without speaking. Once there, they both got out of the car and walked into the backyard. Confronting them was the rusting hulk of a swing set that Spaceman had put up when Robbie was just a little boy and the problems were more easily solved.

Or maybe not. Maybe, Spaceman thought suddenly, those seemingly easy problems hadn't been solved at all by brightly painted swing sets or ball games or whatever, and that was why they had these big problems now. It made him tired just thinking about it.

Robbie sat down on the one surviving swing. It hung so low that his knees reached his chest.

Spaceman strolled the perimeter of the small yard; he sometimes missed having even this much land to walk on and call his own. Not often, but once in a while. "Can I ask you something?" he said at last.

"Ask."

"Why did you do it?"

"Why did I do what?" Robbie asked dully, moving back and forth very slowly.

"What?" Spaceman turned to look at the kid in the glare of the light from the back porch. "Shit, what do you think I'm talking about? Why did you set all those fires?"

"Well, it seemed like a good idea at the time."

Spaceman stalked across the distance between them, one arm raised. Robbie didn't even flinch, just sat looking up at him from that ridiculous position. Spaceman stopped short and lowered his hand. "Sorry." He took a deep breath. "Please, Son, tell me why. I have to know."

Robbie ducked his head and watched his shoes move

through the sparse, muddy grass. "Because," he said in a muffled voice. "Because I wanted somebody to notice me."

"That way?"

"Any way." Robbie looked up at him again and this time Spaceman could see the bright tears washing down his face. "I was scared, Dad. The world was all against me and I was so alone and so scared. I wanted you to save me. But you didn't."

Spaceman was quiet for a long time. Inside the house, Karen was listening to some music, something classical, maybe Mahler. Finally he reached out and touched his son on the shoulder, very lightly. "It's not too late, Robbie," he said quietly. "I can still save you, if you'll just give me the chance."

Somehow Robbie was up out of the damned swing and in his arms. The boy held onto him tightly as Spaceman stroked his back. "It's going to be okay, Son. Really."

Finally, Robbie broke the embrace and stepped back. He wiped his face with one hand. "Thanks. For the burger and stuff."

"Sure. No problem. I'll call. We'll go out for a real dinner while you're here."

"Okay, sure." Robbie looked at him for several seconds, then turned and ran into the house, slamming the door.

Spaceman took one more glance around the place that used to be his—a long time ago, in a different life—and then he left.

19

"**Y**ou can be a very scary son of a bitch."

Lars Morgan just grinned. His damned hair, which he kept forgetting to get cut, was hanging in his face again, and he shoved it back with one hand. The other hand was wrapped around the glass of whiskey. "Me, scary?"

Devlin looked around the dimly lit, moderately crowded Wilshire bar, as if hoping that by seeing other people engaged in normal activity, he could ground himself in something more real than what had happened earlier in the evening. "The way you handled Phillipe Tran. I thought you might really hurt him."

"Not yet. And maybe never, if he cooperates."

"And if he doesn't?"

"Why borrow trouble?" Lars was still smiling.

Devlin searched for the barmaid and signaled her to refill both their glasses. He didn't speak again until she had done so and departed. "I don't know. Maybe it's me. A lot of years have gone by. I've sort of forgotten just what it was like over there. What you were like."

"I was a mean, vicious bastard," Lars said cheerfully.

"True. Very true."

Lars took a sip of his drink. "But I got out alive, Dev. Wasn't that the point? And more than that, I got almost every one of my men out alive, too. All the ones who listened to me, anyway." He raised his glass in a mocking toast. "As a matter of fact, I even got a few dumbass civilians back home in one piece."

"Like a certain bloody stupid picture taker. Who shall remain nameless."

"Right, mate."

Devlin was quiet briefly, then said, "Granted that you were a smashing success in Nam. Did your job just the way they ordered you to and still managed to save yourself and the rest of us. Damn, you were the best. But I guess I just thought that you would have changed since then. Like the rest of us. Softened a little. Maybe even gotten civilized."

"Thanks a lot."

He looked up quickly. "I didn't mean that the way it sounded."

"Okay. Well, I'm sorry to disappoint you, lover. But there is one difference that you seem to have forgotten."

"What?"

"For me, there have been a lot more jungles between then and now. You and the rest pulled yourselves out of that madness. But not me; I'm still there."

Devlin nodded. "By choice."

"Really?" He thought about that. "Well, maybe. But I think that a man likes to do what he's best at."

"I'm not really disagreeing with any of that. It's just that . . . well, like I said, you can be scary."

"For our purposes now, I'd say that's very good."

"I guess so." Devlin was quiet, then he began to smile. "I have an idea."

"What?"

"Let's have a go at the game."

Lars drank. "I was hoping you'd say that." He reached into his pocket and pulled out a quarter, which he tossed quickly into the air. "Call it."

"Heads."

He checked the fall of the coin and shrugged philosophically. "Go to it, old man, your choice."

Devlin got to his feet and began a slow tour of the bar.

This first trip was simply a recon, sizing up the territory, so to speak. When he had reached their table again, he paused.

"Well?" Lars said.

"I'm deciding." He walked off again.

Lars watched, amused, as Devlin approached a well-built redhead in a short, tight yellow dress. She looked like a moderately priced whore.

Devlin squeezed in next to her and leaned close for some conversation. She listened briefly and shook her head, but Lars wasn't worried. No broad in the world could resist Devlin Conway's sky-blue eyes and line of Aussie bullshit. He talked some more and, like always, the broad finally nodded.

They both walked back to the table. "Lars, meet the charming Miss Lydia. She has generously agreed to spend some time with us this evening."

She wore too much eyeshadow and her face was hard-edged, but that was the way Lars liked it. A whore should look like one.

"Nothing generous about it," she said. "You're paying double, since there's two of you."

Devlin lifted his glass and drained it. "Three is the perfect number," he said. "Right, Lars?"

Lars nodded at him.

The motel she led them to was just around the corner from the bar. Devlin paid for the room, shoving a bill through the small window in the bulletproof wall that protected the clerk. Lydia led them up two flights of narrow, dimly lit stairs. This place was the real pits and, again, Lars was pleased.

The rules of their game were strict. The winner of the toss not only got to choose the woman in question, but also had the first go round with her. Lars, meanwhile, sat in the only chair the room offered, a grimy, overstuffed relic of another era. He snapped a can of beer from the six-pack they'd picked up on the way over, popped it open, and lighted a cigarette.

The room was dark, except for the vivid glow cast by a large neon sign just outside the window. As Lydia and Devlin undressed quickly, the light changed from red to blue and back again every few seconds, casting a strange glow over the room and its occupants.

It was funny, but even though they hadn't played the game since that night in San Diego, Lars could still anticipate how things would go between the two on the bed. Devlin's screwing technique was predictable. Of course, Lars decided ruefully, his own sexual habits were probably just as reliable. In a way, it was reassuring to know that Devlin hadn't changed.

For thirty minutes or so, he drank beer and smoked as he watched the two red-blue-red shapes roll around on the bed together. Finally, Devlin raised himself over the woman and plunged into her. Lars figured that he could have predicted the exact number of strokes required before Devlin stiffened, gasped once, and came. The woman knew her job; she gave a soft moan at just the right moment.

Even though the whole thing had an air of comfortable familiarity to it, Lars still felt a sudden rush of heat at the final moment.

While Devlin caught his breath, Lars stood and undressed. He handed Devlin a half-full can of beer and a partly smoked cigarette, then took his place on the bed. At the urging of Lars' hands, Lydia slid down his body and took him into her mouth. The sheets smelled of her, and of sweat and semen; the dampness and the odors made Lars hard almost at once. That was the danger of getting the second helping: Finishing didn't take long under those circumstances. He was peripherally aware of Devlin across the room, watching. Or maybe not watching, but there.

When Lars was done with the woman, they paid her off

and she left. Since there was still some beer to drink and the room was paid for, Lars stayed where he was. Devlin dragged the chair closer, propping his feet on the bed, and they started talking about old times.

Blue was in bed, but not asleep, when the call came. "Hello?" He recognized the tentative sound of his own voice and that irritated him.

"This you, Blue?"

"It's me." He scooted up on the pillows a little.

"Well, good. I called before, but there wasn't no answer."

"I had to work late." Blue reached over toward the nightstand and picked up a half-full glass of wine. Just a simple Chablis. That wasn't really like drinking.

"Yeah? You work, huh? Even with all that dough?"

"Sure. I mean, you have to work, right?"

"Not me. I been laid off for ten months now."

"That's too bad."

"Well, it wasn't like this was the first time or nothing. Actually, I've had a kind of hard time keeping jobs. It's funny, but the last time I worked really steady was in the service."

"I'm sorry to hear that." The sparkling gold liquid felt good going down.

"So what kind of work you do, buddy? Your old man, he's like a big shit in electronics or something right?"

"Computers. He was into computers."

"Jeez, yeah. Fucking computers. That's the place to be today. All the fucking money's in those babies."

Blue stretched. "Well, that might be true, but I'm not in computers. I'm a cop."

"You shittin' me? That the truth?"

"It's true."

"I'll be damned." There was a pause, then the voice said suspiciously, "You're not tracing this call or something, are you?"

"No, of course not. Why would I do that?"

"That's the kind of thing a fucking cop would do."

"I'm not tracing the call. Forget that." Blue wondered why he hadn't even thought of trying something like a trace. "What kind of work are you into?"

"Didn't I just say I was laid off? Aren't you even listening? My only job is going down to the fucking welfare office once a week."

"Before that."

"Lotta things. Mostly, I was on the line."

"The line?"

"Making cars, Loot. Doing my bit for the good old American dream."

"That's good."

"Good? You think?"

"Don't you?"

There was a harsh laugh. "I think that none of it matters very fucking much. Not one goddamned little bit, in fact. I go through the motions with the damned welfare and the damned union and you go through the same motions with the damned pig department, but none of it fucking matters. Just a lot of motion, that's all."

Blue shook his head. "That's not true."

"Ahh, Loot, cut the crap, willya? You don't hafta to play the game with me. I know you. I seen you fall apart and I knew what was happening, 'cause I was fucking falling apart, too. Don't you know the truth of it yet?"

"What truth?"

"All the king's horses and all the king's men can't put us poor bastards back together again."

Blue very carefully replaced the receiver in the cradle.

20

It was almost dawn. The grey sky was beginning to brighten just a little, but the street outside the motel was still almost deserted. He leaned out the window to see if the clouds looked like they were threatening more rain. "This frigging weather is going to make me crazy pretty soon," he said.

"More than you already are?"

Lars lifted a finger in the other man's direction, then finished buttoning his shirt. They were both in rotten shape. They had talked almost all night, finally falling into a drugged-like sleep that lasted only about an hour. It left them bleary-eyed and speaking in rough-edged voices.

Devlin went into the grimy bathroom, eyed the toilet doubtfully, and decided just to splash some cold water into his face. It didn't help much. "Hell," he said glumly, staring into the cracked mirror. "I have a meeting with a critic from the *Times* in a few hours."

"Oh, well, aren't all you artistic types supposed to be like dissipated or something?"

"I'm definitely that. Or something." He walked back into the other room. "And what about you?"

"Me?"

'What happens next?'

"I've got some feelers out. People I need to talk to."

"Good luck." Devlin didn't sound very optimistic.

Lars pulled his jacket on, automatically patting the pocket to be sure that the gun was still in place. The gesture was so ingrained that he wasn't even aware of doing it. "Let's get out of here."

Outside, there was a faint promise of maybe some sunshine later in the day, and Lars felt his mood lift higher as they headed back to where the car was parked. "I could do with some chow," he said. "You want to get some breakfast?" He was feeling really up. This had been a good time and he was reluctant to have it end.

Lars knew very well that things could get—would get—pretty rough before long and this would be a good memory. All his life, he tried to collect the nice times and save them inside. There weren't so many. "What about some pancakes?" he offered.

He knew better than to let his defenses down, even for a moment, but nobody was perfect. Lars didn't see the man step out of the alley, but something in Devlin's face alerted him. Before he could react, however, there was the unmistakable pressure of a gun barrel jammed firmly into his spine. He stayed very still, silently willing Devlin to do the same.

"Wolf, you're making some very important people nervous. They don't like being nervous, so it would be good for you to stop."

Devlin was so quiet that he scarcely even seemed to be breathing. Apparently by deliberation, he was ignoring the man, staring instead at Lars.

Lars smiled faintly, although the creep with the gun couldn't see him. "Hey, buddy, all I want is a meet. Just to talk."

"Nobody wants to talk to you, Wolf. Nobody even wants to hear your name again. Got that?"

"Got it. Fine. No problem."

"So I can tell my people that we have an understanding, right?"

"Sure thing."

The pressure of the gun was gone. "Don't turn around," he warned.

"Fine." Lars waited another second, then, without even pulling the gun out of his pocket, turned and fired once. The man fell like a rock and died on the way to the ground.

Lars let go of the gun and pulled his hand out. "Maybe now those assholes will talk to me, right?"

Devlin looked away, taking several deep breaths.

"You okay, Dev?"

He finally turned back to face Lars. "Sure. Sure. It's just that the sight of violent death before my first cup of coffee in the morning always gives me a queasy feeling."

"He was one of the bad guys."

"No doubt."

Lars bent over the dead man, grabbing him by both ankles, and dragged him into the alley. He shoved the body behind a line of garbage cans. "Which is actually quite appropriate, if you think about it," he said over his shoulder.

Devlin didn't say anything.

When Lars had the body completely hidden, they began to walk again, more quickly this time, in an unspoken but mutual desire to distance themselves from what had just happened.

Once they were safely in the car, Devlin leaned back against the seat and closed his eyes. "Christ Almighty, you're one cold son of a bitch, Lars."

Lars had the key ready to shove into the ignition, but he paused, looking at Devlin. "I'm damned sorry."

"Sorry?"

"That you don't approve of me."

"It's not a matter of approval. Maybe I even admire you, but that doesn't change the fact that you're a very frightening man."

"You're frightened?" His voice rang with disbelief.

Devlin opened his eyes and turned to meet his gaze. "Not of you personally, of course. But of what surrounds you. The danger. It seems like the air stinks of it."

"That's the way I live."

"My God, how do you stand it? You should be a raving maniac."

Lars just said, "Do you want out? If you do, just say so."

There was a long silence.

Then Devlin shook his head. "No. No, I don't want out." He spoke firmly, but wearily.

Lars grinned his relief. "You ready for that coffee now?"

21

They were sitting in a tacky diner on Ninth Street. Spaceman was actually eating, having ordered the lunch special, which turned out to be a greasy hamburger. What made it special, apparently, was the bag of undoubtedly soggy potato chips served on the side.

Blue, who believed in being grateful for even the smallest of favors, was very glad to be sitting across the room from where his partner was eating. And eating, unbelievably, with apparent relish. As for Blue himself, he wasn't even sure that he wanted to drink the cup of coffee he'd ordered simply to avoid being conspicuous.

They were sitting apart not to spare Blue's sensibilities, but because Spaceman was here to meet one of his snitches. Snitches were a breed inclined, perhaps justifiably, toward a certain amount of paranoia. While a stoolie would talk openly with his own particular cop, there was some reluctance to feel outnumbered. So Blue was sitting at the counter, pretending like he'd just decided to drop into the Black Hole of Calcutta for a cup of the great java, and at the same time trying to keep his french cuffs out of any of the unidentifiable puddles that dotted the countertop.

Spaceman straightened a little as the diner door opened again. The new customer was a very tall, almost painfully thin black man. He wore a shiny green suit, a Robin Hood hat with a small red feather, and yellow plastic sunglasses.

He walked directly to Spaceman's booth and sat down. The two men talked briefly, while Blue tried to watch and not look as if he was watching.

He was startled when Spaceman suddenly raised a hand to wave him over, but after a moment, he slid from the stool and went. He left the coffee behind.

"My old buddy Roy here thought that you might as well join us," Spaceman said dryly.

"He made me for a cop?"

Roy's laugh had a rusty, unused sound to it. "Hell, boy," he said. "The way you dressed, I knew you had to be a fag, a pimp, or some kind of crazy Hollywood-type cop. Ain't no pansy in his right mind gonna come in here. And you much too vanilla to be a pimp in this neighborhood. So by process of elimination, I figure out that you must be a noble defender of the public safety."

Blue frowned, glancing down at his new Giorgio Armani sportscoat and striped shirt. "What's wrong with the way I'm dressed?"

"Nothing," Spaceman muttered. "You look beautiful. Sit the hell down and let Roy tell us what he knows."

Blue slid in next to Spaceman and kept his mouth shut. Never having spent much time on the streets before his fairly recent shift into homicide, he didn't have any snitches to call his own yet. Well, there were a couple of members of the city administration he knew from his days in public relations. They sometimes called to shoot the bull about what was going on in City Hall, but that probably didn't count.

Roy helped himself to a chip. It was soggy. "I don't have much," he said. "Mostly just a lot of hopeful talk on the streets."

"Hopeful talk about what?"

" 'Bout mebbe it's gonna be a white Christmas. Or a white New Year, at least. Big blizzard supposed to hit the city. Good days be coming, is what they say."

"Who is they?"

Roy smiled, showing two gold teeth, one on either side of

his mouth, like bookends. "All those poor, simpleminded folk who still believes in Santy Claus and the good fairy."

"What else?"

Roy took his time before answering, pulling out a long black cigar and going through the ritual of lighting it. "The way I hear it, there's a new supplier coming to town. From the east."

"New York?" Spaceman said.

"Not that east, fool. I mean the Orient."

"Which might explain Hua," Spaceman said to Blue. He had finally finished the hamburger and so naturally he reached for a cigarette. Blue tried to lean as far away as he could from the impenetrable cloud of smoke rising from the booth. "But this talk about a new supplier," Spaceman said. "Won't that upset some people?"

"Not the folks what plays with their noses, it won't."

"Not them. I mean Papa D. This territory has been his for a long time. The last fool who tried to open up as an independent upset Papa a lot." He glanced at Blue, smiling faintly. "We found that turkey in the old zoo. And in Inglewood. And even a little bit in Malibu, I think, although that piece was hard to identify. No prints on that particular part of a person's anatomy." He snickered at the memory.

Roy nodded. "What you say is true. But in this case, I have heard that Papa D. is making some kind of deal. Maybe the old man is feeling his age and looking to retire."

"Maybe."

Roy unwound his length and stood. "That's all I got, Spaceman, and the horses are at the gate."

"Okay, thanks." Spaceman took a folded bill from his shirt pocket and slid it across the table.

Roy reached for it.

But Spaceman kept two fingers on the money. "By the way, from now on, you can consider a call from Detective Maguire here the same as a call from me."

Roy's gaze flickered over Blue for a moment, then he

nodded. "Your man is my man." The money was released and Roy was gone.

Blue waved the lingering cigar smoke out of his face. "Doesn't he take a chance meeting you in public like this?"

"Roy? Nah, he's a bookie. As far as anybody else knows, he's my bookie."

"Is he?"

Spaceman only grinned.

They paid the tab and left the diner. Blue stopped beside the car. "About my clothes," he said.

"Forget it. You can't help yourself."

"The thing is, I'm having dinner with Sharon after we get off." He felt like a damned school kid, admitting to having a date with the head cheerleader or something.

Spaceman held up a V-for-victory sign.

Blue wanted to tell him that he and Sharon were a long way from victory, but instead he just shrugged and got into the car.

22

Toby was swimming half-heartedly, his thoughts a long way from the pleasant surroundings of the Century West Club. Despite his complete lack of attention or interest, he did the usual number of laps back and forth across the pool. By this time, it was pure instinct. The old self-preservation thing. A man past thirty didn't keep the body of a twenty-five-year-old by shirking the essentials.

He finally finished and pulled himself up out of the water. Lars Morgan handed him a towel. Not showing his surprise, Toby sat on the cool tile and began to dry himself. "How the hell did you get in here?" he asked.

"It wasn't easy. You picked a pretty ritzy place to sweat in."

He knew the club was expensive. It was the favorite of the young professionals who inhabited the heights of Century City, and more than an occasional celebrity. Toby shrugged. "Yeah, well, I could go to the Y. The sweat would be the same, I guess, but my psyche would suffer. This place is an indulgence. Someplace I can go to get away from it all." He glanced at Lars. "Usually, at least," he said ruefully. "What do you want anyway?"

"I have a visit to make and I just wanted some company."

"Is this going to be anything like the visit you and Conway made to Phillipe Tran?"

Lars was playing with his car keys. "You saw Dev?"

Toby shook his head. "We talked, is all." He stood to finish drying his legs. "Hell, we're both in this thing. I just thought that we should touch base with each other." He could read in the superficially placid grey eyes exactly what was bugging Lars. "Don't worry, Wolf, we weren't plotting behind your back."

Lars was obviously irritated that his thoughts had been so transparent and the face closed up even more. "I know that, damnit." He picked up the discarded wet towel and threw it at Toby. "Go get dressed."

"Who are we going to see?" Toby pressed.

"Just Tran again. We might have to be a little more, ah, persuasive this time is all."

"And you figure that I can persuade better than Devlin?"

Lars grinned, his good humor restored. "Hell, lover boy, just flex your pecs at the little creep and he'll fall down in fear."

Toby flicked the towel at him, then headed for the locker room to change.

The only customers in the vegetable store when they entered were a couple of old Viet women, dressed entirely in black and chattering softly in their own language. Ignoring them, Lars took one of the empty carts and pushed it as he led the way up the main aisle.

Toby followed. He was now wearing what might be called Beverly Hills macho—there were women, including his scheduled client for this afternoon, who got off on the battered leather bomber jacket and the button-fly 501 Levis. Toby was mildly bemused by what was going on here. Real life had disappeared, replaced, it seemed, by bad melodrama. Once upon a time, he'd had a client, a plump redhead, whose husband owned a disco and was supposedly part of the Vegas mob. That brief relationship was Toby's closest brush with the so-called underworld.

Discounting, of course, his days in the street gangs of

Chicago. Now, however, he was caught up in something more dangerous, although it was still far from clear to him exactly what that something was.

Phillipe Tran was standing at the far end of the aisle. He held a yellow garden hose in one hand, idly directing a fine spray over a bin of dark green, waxy cucumbers. He did not seem to notice their approach.

At a nod from Lars, Toby held back slightly, arms akimbo. He tried to look silently menacing and felt like a damned fool. Then he thought back twenty-five years or so, remembering a scared Okie farm kid, suddenly orphaned and dumped on the streets of the Windy City. Get tough or die, his uncle said. And so he got tough.

It had been a long time since those days, but the memory was still sharp. He felt as if one layer of his soul was being slowly stripped away—the part of him that was a soft and pretty toy for all the rich bitches in the city—and underneath there was still a punk with the motorcycle boots and switchblade. Or maybe it was a more recent incarnation being revealed—the bloody and bloodied soldier with his precious M-16.

It occurred to Toby that he didn't know who the hell he really was.

Lars had parked the cart so that it blocked any possible escape, then stepped forward to put a hand on Tran's shoulder. Startled, the man jumped spastically. The hose jerked and water sprayed sideways, almost soaking Lars, who managed to step away quickly enough to avoid getting wet.

Toby was glad that the water had missed, because there was something about the look on Lars' face that worried him a little. Something that seemed to say Phillipe Tran was walking on a dangerous edge.

"Hello, there, Phillipe." The pleasant, buddy-buddy tone was belied by the stony eyes. "Don't get so nervous. It's just me. And you probably remember good old Tobias here."

Tran glanced beyond Lars, to where Toby stood, but neither man spoke.

"We're here to talk some more about the diamonds," Lars said, still sounding friendly.

"Those damned diamonds again. I told you before that I don't know anything about them." Tran bent over and reached behind the bin to turn off the water.

As he straightened, Lars moved. The side of his hand jabbed sharply into Tran's gut. Tran grunted and clutched at his stomach. "Boy, I am getting sick and tired of screwing around with you. No more fun and games." The voice was cold and hollow-sounding now; the heat of anger would have been far less frightening.

Toby glanced around, but suddenly the old ladies were gone and he was alone with Tran and Lars. That wasn't an especially comforting thought; it reminded him too much of the old days.

Somebody had to break through the nearly visible tension that was surrounding the three of them or what happened might be very bad. Shit, Toby thought, it was up to him. Again. Sometimes no one, not even Conway, could pull Lars Morgan's chain and keep him under control like he could. God only knew why. Toby just knew that there were a number of people from the old days who were alive only because of him. Not to mention a whole damned village that came very close to being torched.

"Tran, let's get to it. The unhappy truth is that you're dealing here with a couple of very hard cases. It seems to me like there's two possible ways you can play this hand you seem to have been dealt. There's the easy way and the rough way. I know what my choice would be, but then I don't like pain much."

Lars shot him a mildly irritated look, which he ignored.

Tran picked up an orange and tossed it from hand to hand several times. "The diamonds belonged to my father," he said finally. "What's in this for me if I cooperate?"

"Ten thousand," Lars said.

"Fifty."

Lars just laughed.

Tran glanced again at Toby, as if hoping to find an ally there, but Toby only shrugged. After one more moment, Tran gave in. "I've heard some gossip," he said. "Old names from home."

"What old names?"

He was still trying to play it cagey, not commit himself too far until he could see just what the score was. "Maybe Ky?" he suggested.

Lars spit across the aisle. "To hell with Ky," he said harshly. "I know he's not in this and you know it, too."

Tran bit his lip as he realized that a bluff wasn't going to work. "Okay, look, I want to go along with you. After all, you were my father's partners, right? But I need to talk to some people first. I mean, you cannot expect me to, ah, burn all my bridges, can you?"

Lars was quiet, except for a soft whistle as he thought it over. "Twenty-four hours," he said at last. "I'm running out of time fast here, which means that you're running out even faster. Tell me what I want to know then or it won't be nice what happens to General Tran's little boy. You capice?"

In the melting pot that was Los Angeles, Tran understood and he nodded to indicate that he capiced all too clearly.

Back on the sidewalk in front of the store, Lars stopped to light a cigarette. "You did good in there, Tobias," he said, apparently forgetting his earlier irritation. "Just enough menace coming across."

"Takes no brains to have balls," Toby muttered. The words were something he'd seen scribbled on the wall in the men's room of one of the city's fanciest clubs. He glanced at his watch. "You know, boss, we don't have this frigging fortune yet, and I'm supposed to be working in twenty minutes."

Lars grinned, but rather surprisingly passed up the opportunity to make a crack about Toby's line of work as they got into the car.

23

Sharon Engels, of the medical examiner's office, had a serious expression on her face. Her brow wrinkled slightly as she tried the wine. Then she nodded. "You have an unerring palate, sir," she said lightly.

Everything the two of them had said so far during the evening had been said lightly. If things got any jollier, Blue was afraid he might throw up.

He'd been hoping that a romantic dinner would take the edge off their anger. Then he discarded that word. No, it wasn't anger that he felt. It was more like a bad case of hurt feelings, and he sort of thought that Sharon was experiencing the same thing. The whole thing was utterly stupid, like a couple of children squabbling in the sandbox, and it had kept them apart for nearly two weeks.

But how could he miss with dinner at a place with a name like Romeo and Juliet?

Still, he had to admit, things had not been an unqualified success since their rendezvous in the parking lot. They seemed to be dancing around one another, like boxers afraid of a body blow.

Sharon was apparently totally involved in reading the menu. "I've missed you, Blue," she said suddenly, not looking up.

"Me, too. I mean, I've missed you." Smooth, Maguire, nice

to see that all those Saturday mornings spent in Miss Pud-
dingham's charm school hadn't been wasted.

"We've been a couple of real dopes to blow all this time
pouting."

"It's not too late." He hoped.

She shrugged. "I leave in two days."

"That soon?" Blue took a drink of the perfect, one hundred and fifty dollar-a-bottle-wine, but now the taste seemed
just a little off. "You haven't thought about not going?"

"Thought about it?" She toyed with a strand of untamed
hair. "Yes, Blue, I did think about it."

"And?" He tried to make the one word sound casual.

Across the room, someone laughed loudly.

Sharon shook her head. "And I'd be a complete idiot to
pass up this opportunity."

"I know that."

"Well, then?"

At times like this, Blue regretted his decision to give up
smoking. The rituals involved in the consumption of tobacco
could be used very nicely to fill awkward moments. As it
was, all he could do was swallow some more wine and, like
her, pretend to study the menu. Finally he gave up. "Look,
Shar, I know how important this is to you. I'm glad the
chance came. And if this were a perfect world—or if I were
the perfect new era man—that would be an end to it. But the
world isn't perfect and I'm not even close. So while part of
me, the modern, feminist-male part, says good for you and
go for it, there's another part that feels . . . rejected. Hurt, I
guess, because you'd rather go off to do your own thing
instead of staying here with me. There."

"Well, that's honest. Alan Alda would be proud of you."

He smiled grimly. "So how many points do I get for
honesty?"

"There is a solution," she said with a smile of her own.

"What?"

"You could always quit your job and come with me."

He was genuinely startled. "Quit? Oh, no. I mean, no, Shar, I couldn't do that."

"Of course not. Because as much as you care for me—and I know you do care, a lot—you love your job more."

Blue nodded.

"So you understand how I feel."

"Yes, of course." He sighed, more resigned than sad now. "I guess what bothers me most is that what we have is so new yet, so untested, I'm afraid it won't be able to survive this. Johns Hopkins is a long ways from here and a year is a long time. I don't know if we can come through unscathed."

Sharon was quiet for a moment, then she shrugged. "I guess we'll find out."

At that, some of the tension seemed to fade away and they smiled at one another. Blue cheered up a little. Whatever happened, there was still the rest of this night to look forward to.

One thought came to him: At least, if he slept at Sharon's, the only phone calls he would get would be from Spaceman.

After signing out, Spaceman thought about maybe driving out to Azusa to see if Lainie wanted to catch some dinner, but he knew that she would be rushed and harried and say no. Rejection was something he definitely didn't need at the moment.

Or he could have called Robbie, but playing the role of Great White Father didn't appeal much this evening either. So instead of doing anything, he just went into Joe's and ordered a burger to eat as he read the *Times*. Joe was engrossed in a television Christmas special with Debbie Boone, so he was left blissfully alone.

Just as Spaceman was finishing his meal, the door opened and Petrie came in. Lew Petrie, a husky black detective, was one of Spaceman's former partners. That, in itself, was a large and varied group. Petrie, however, was a rarity in the crowd, being an ex-partner with whom Kowalski still had a cordial relationship. He didn't even hold it against Space-man that he'd lost ten dollars in the office pool betting on how long the Kowalski/Maguire partnership would endure. Everybody lost money on that.

Now, beginning to be bored with his own company, Spaceman folded the newspaper eagerly. "What's up, Lew?"

Petrie slid onto the stool next to his. "Same old shit," he replied in a soft Alabama accent. "The never-ending battle against sin in the big city."

"Is that what we're supposed to be doing?" Spaceman said skeptically. "Fighting sin?"

Petrie shrugged. Without bothering to look at the menu, he ordered a chilidog and a vanilla milk shake. "And I'm in a hurry," he said to Joe. "There's a stiff waiting to be posted and I want to watch."

Spaceman tossed the paper aside. "You'll do anything for a good time, you sicko."

The black man glanced at him. "Hell, it's your fault. You got me into the habit back when we worked together."

Spaceman silently accepted the blame. He always tried to attend the postmortems on his cases whenever possible. It was a sometimes sickening, always unhappy business, but it served to motivate him to track down whatever bastard was responsible.

Petrie took a huge bite of the messy hotdog and chewed briefly before speaking again. "By the way, this stiff is an old friend of yours."

"Who's that?"

"Teddy Vacarro."

"No shit? Old Teddy the Toad?" Spaceman shook his head in mock grief. "What happened?"

"Who knows? He just turned up in an alley today. Shot."

"That's a real shame."

Petrie snickered. "Yeah, I can tell you're all broken up about it."

"Hey, I am. I mean, you don't find real low-down slime

bags like old Teddy around much these days. What do you have on it?"

Chili dripped from Petrie's chin; he grabbed a napkin and wiped at it. "Not much. The bullet passed right through him and came out the other side, which was pretty messy. Not too banged up. The bullet, that is. Teddy was banged up enough to be cold stone dead."

Spaceman drained his coffee cup. "It could have been something simple," he said doubtfully. "Like a mugging."

Petrie shook his head. "His wallet and watch were there. Besides, not too many muggers in that neighborhood use Walther P-38s."

In the act of reaching for his wallet, Spaceman paused. "A Walther? No shit?"

"We think. The perp left a casing behind. Lab's pretty sure, and I think they're right."

Spaceman went ahead and pulled his wallet out, extracting a couple of bills. "Would you mind a little company at the post?"

Petrie looked at him, surprised. "What's going on?"

"Maguire and I have two stiffs, both maybe offed with a Walther."

Petrie thought about that. "Any tie to Vacarro?"

Spaceman grimaced. "So far in this case, nothing ties to anything."

The last of the chilidog vanished. "Well, let's go watch them cut on poor old Teddy." He grinned. "If it works out, son, I'd be more than glad to turn him over to you."

Spaceman was glum as he followed Petrie out of the café. While Blue Maguire was making it with a good-looking broad, he'd be watching the pathologist fool around inside Teddy the Toad's body.

" 'Tis the season to be jolly," he muttered to Petrie's broad back.

24

Devlin Conway walked into Nate 'n Al's Delicatessen and stopped to check out the room, which was busy as usual. There was a short line of customers waiting to be seated, but then he spotted Toby. They ran into one another several times a year, when he was in town, usually at some ritzy cocktail party or other, where Devlin was playing minor celebrity and Toby was being paid to be charming.

Toby saw him and raised one hand in a lazy greeting.

Devlin slowly made his way through the crowd and joined him. "You're looking fit and prosperous," he said, dropping into the comfortable booth.

Toby just smiled behind his sunglasses.

A waiter appeared. Devlin ordered lox and bagels and, desperately, coffee, while Toby settled for two scrambled eggs, grapefruit juice and dry toast. "I was three pounds over my fighting weight this morning," he explained somewhat sheepishly.

Devlin didn't say much until his coffee was in front of him. Even then, he took a healthy portion of the strong black brew first. "You said it was important that we should get together, Toby," he said finally. "Why?"

"I just thought that maybe we should talk face-to-face. Without Lars."

Devlin frowned.

Toby sipped grapefruit juice. "Don't worry," he said,

sounding exasperated. "I'm not planning a mutiny or anything. I'm just a little concerned. Lars seems . . ." His hand moved back and forth in a seesaw motion.

"When didn't he?"

"True. But this is pretty bad." Toby ran a hand through his hair and smiled absently at a passing woman. "Besides, behavior that was appropriate in some places doesn't go down so good in Los Angeles."

Devlin considered, trying to decide how much he could say without compromising Lars. Could Toby be trusted? But he had to confide in someone, and Toby was part of this—so apparently Lars trusted him. Still, he probed a little. "How committed are you to this? To Lars?"

Toby didn't answer quickly. And when he did speak, it was with obvious care in his choice of words. "When this whole thing started,'" he said, "I was sort of on the fence. Could have gone either way, you know what I mean?"

Devlin nodded.

"But the more I think about it, about all the money, the more I want this to work. And besides, in a way, the stones really belong to us, don't they?"

"One could say so."

"So I'm in. All the way." He shrugged. "I know all the things there are to be worried about. I think."

Devlin stared at the tabletop. "He killed a man."

"Lars?"

"Yes, Lars, of course."

Toby took the glasses off and cleaned them carefully on his napkin. "Who?" he said, the sudden brightness making him squint a little.

Devlin inhaled, then let it out very slowly. "I think the guy was some kind of hood. Or whatever they're called these days. And he did put a gun on Lars first, so . . . ."

"So maybe it was justified?"

"Well, I have to think so, right?"

"Or else?"

Devlin shook his head. "There is no 'or else.' Not in this situation."

"Because it's Morgan you mean."

"Maybe. Yes, I guess."

Toby replaced his glasses, covering eyes that tended to be too candid. "You're a very loyal friend."

"Am I?"

They stayed quiet as the breakfast was delivered. When they were alone again, Devlin poured sugar into his coffee. "It's just complicated, Toby. Everybody needs some kind of anchor. What I do, with my work, is grab hold of reality and keep it on film. That's for other people. It gives them something to hold on to. An anchor. But I need something for myself, too."

Toby sprinkled salt and pepper on his eggs. "And your anchor in real life is Lars Morgan?" he said skeptically.

"We've been friends for a long time. And we've been through a lot together. You were there, too, you remember." Then he smiled, vaguely self-mocking. "No doubt you're right. It's not a smart choice. But I seem to be stuck with it."

"I guess we both are now," Toby said. "God have mercy on our souls."

Devlin raised his coffee cup toward Toby. "Well, I'm glad you're with us, anyway," he said. "When my back is to the bloody wall, I think you'll come in much more useful than any deity."

Toby smiled and took a bit of egg. "Besides," he said around the food, "I'm the only one with guts enough to at least try to sit on Morgan, right?"

Devlin wanted to object to that, but after a moment, he just shrugged and picked up a bagel.

25

The Vietnam Veterans Center reminded Blue, rather ironically, he thought, of the refugee center they'd visited the other day. This place, too, was a rundown building with a crooked sign on the door and the same vibes of despair and confusion coming off it.

When they opened the door and stepped inside, their ears were immediately assaulted by the sound of a stereo blasting the ancient sounds of the Jefferson Airplane. A man was sitting at a card table, reading. Wild black hair reached his shoulders and his beard was an untamed bush. He wore jeans, a teeshirt proclaiming that life was more fun with Coke, and a battered fatigue jacket. The impression was one of a museum display: rebel, circa the late 1960s.

A look around the room reinforced the feelings of similarity between the two places. The walls here were also plastered with flyers and urgent announcements. Spaceman stepped over to the cheap stereo and turned the volume down until the music was just a whisper.

For the first time, the man looked up from his Tom Robbins book. "What's the matter?" he asked. "You don't like music?"

"I love music," Spaceman replied pleasantly. "But I like conversation, too."

He stared at them. "Cops, right?"

Spaceman pretended dismay. "We have to rethink our

undercover disguises, Blue," he said. "The look doesn't seem to be working."

Blue smiled faintly. "I'm Maguire," he said. "That's Kowalski."

"Milt Duncan. What's the hassle?"

"No hassle. Just a few simple questions."

"Cops never have simple questions." There was hostility in the words, but there was mostly weariness.

"Hey," Blue said, "don't get so uptight. We're only a couple of vets trying to make a living."

"Right," Duncan said, still annoyed, but relaxing a little.

Blue took out the picture from Hua's apartment. "You know this man?"

Duncan glanced quickly at it. "Which one?"

Blue sighed. "Let's make it easy. The American."

Duncan took the picture from him for a closer look. Blue turned around and began to read some of the flyers on the wall. Most of them seemed to be concerned with job hunting, rock concerts, drug abuse, and rallies to protest Agent Orange.

Duncan tossed the picture onto the table. "Don't know him."

"You sure?" Spaceman said, moving closer.

"As sure as I can be."

"How about the name Wolf? Probably a nickname."

"Wolf?" He chewed his lower lip for a moment. "Maybe in Nam. You know, stories go around. There were guys who made real reps for themselves. Maybe there was a guy named Wolf. But I don't know anything about him."

Blue's attention was caught by a bright yellow poster thumbtacked to the wall. He knew the Addison Gallery, had purchased some paintings and prints from it over the years. He seemed to remember an invitation, somewhere in his pile of recent mail, to the opening of this show featuring Vietnam photographs.

Then he put that aside and turned to Duncan again. "Ever have any drug problems around here?"

Duncan looked at him blandly. "Depends on what you mean by problems."

"Any dealing?"

"No."

"Would you tell me if there were?"

"What do you think?"

Blue only smiled.

Duncan shook his head, tangling the black hair even more. "Listen, man, we're here to help the vets. Our brothers. Nobody else gives a flying fuck about us or our problems. Not the government or the so-called good people of the country. They only want us all to go away and stop reminding them that this frigging country once lost a war."

Blue thought suddenly of his late-night caller. "What kind of problems do you see in here?"

"All kinds of shit. PTSD. Guys strung out from drugs they got in the VA. Agent Orange. We see it all."

Spaceman was already edging toward the door. "But you haven't seen the guy in the picture?"

"Nope, can't say I have."

"Thanks." Blue retrieved the photograph, noticing a jar for contributions on the table; it contained only a few bucks. He took out his wallet and added a fifty to the meager collection.

"Thanks," Duncan said.

He shrugged and started after Spaceman.

"Hey, buddy," Duncan said.

"What?"

"You wanna jack the music for me?"

Blue stepped back to the stereo and swiveled the volume knob until Jim Morrison's voice crashed into the room.

Duncan nodded and picked up his book again.

The Porsche looked right at home on Doheny Road in Beverly Hills. The house they were visiting resembled a castle, complete with turrets and a large, lush lawn. There was a gate and also a guard, but since they had called for an appointment, he waved them through without delay.

Spaceman peered through the windshield as they parked. "Whoever it was that said crime doesn't pay didn't know what the hell he was talking about," he muttered.

Blue turned the engine off and pocketed the keys. "So that's Papa D.'s house. Hell, you'd think the president of General Motors lived there, instead of just a crook."

"Oh, Papa's not your everyday kind of scumbag, Blue. He's a very crafty old bastard. Been around since just after the dawn of civilization."

They got out of the car. Spaceman dropped his cigarette onto the otherwise spotless driveway and stepped on it, while Blue straightened his beige silk tie. "I know him, by the way," the blond said.

Spaceman looked surprised. "What? You and Delvecchio?"

They started up the long brick walk that led to the house. "Well, don't make it sound like we went to the junior prom together," Blue said irritably. "We just sat at the same table a couple times at some Rotary Club things."

"Ahh, the wonderful things that happen to you lucky stiffs in public relations."

"Yeah, it was exciting, all right. But the good days are over now and for my sins I'm here on the mean streets with you, Kowalski."

"So what'd you think of him?"

"Delvecchio? I thought he was a gabby, boring old man. Just one of the crowd. He complimented me for working on a fine police department. I asked him to pass the butter." Blue paused. "He knew my father."

That earned him another look.

Blue sighed. "My father knew everybody, Spaceman, so don't make a big thing out of it."

Spaceman shook his head, then cleared his throat and spit into the sculptured bushes that lined the front of the house. "Bastard," he said, without specifying who the epithet applied to. He gestured toward the door. "Do your stuff, Mr. Public Relations."

Blue rang the bell.

Almost immediately the door was opened by a plump Mexican woman wearing a black dress and a ruffled white apron. She was reluctant to admit that Señor Delvecchio was at home or even that they had an appointment. But finally her hostility melted under some of Blue's soft Spanish persuasion.

"Uno momento," she said, closing the door and leaving them on the steps.

Spaceman reached for another cigarette. "So what are your plans for the big day?" he said with unaccustomed amiability.

"Big day?"

"Christmas, you idiot."

Blue shrugged. "I never make plans. I'm a spontaneous kind of guy."

Spaceman gave him a quizzical look, but before he could say anything, the door opened again. The maid was still frowning, but she let them in and led the way down a seemingly endless hall. Finally they reached a set of sliding glass doors.

They stepped through, onto a screened patio. Dominic Delvecchio, about eighty, with a shock of white hair and nut-brown wrinkled skin, was sitting in a cushioned chair, watching a small color television. He wore a maroon satin robe. Nearby was a small table that held a glass of orange juice.

They stood there until the soap opera broke for a commercial. Delvecchio touched a button and the sound vanished. "You haven't been coming to the meetings lately," he said. The voice was surprisingly strong, sounding as if it should have belonged to a younger, bigger man.

"I beg your pardon?" Blue said.

"You're Maguire, right? Hank Maguire's boy? I haven't seen you at the Rotary meetings lately."

"You remember me?"

The old man snorted. "Hell, you won't get far in life if you don't make a point of remembering names and faces."

"Yes, sir. Well, I don't go to those meetings anymore, because they shifted me from public relations to homicide."

"I see. What brings you here then?"

Spaceman, purely for show, yanked out his notebook and flipped it open. "We're here to talk about one of your employees. A Mr. Theodore Vacarro. Known to his friends, if any, as Teddy the Toad."

Delvecchio said nothing. In fact, he gave no indication of even having heard Spaceman's words.

"The Toad is dead, Papa, and we think maybe his death has something to do with a big drug deal about to happen."

"I'm an old man. The world behaves very strangely these days."

"Bullshit," Spaceman said.

Blue shook his head, smiling. "Excuse my partner," he said. "Diplomacy has never been his strong suit." The words themselves were polite enough, but everyone could hear the steel beneath them. Even Delvecchio had to realize that the apology was absolutely insincere.

Delvecchio lifted a hand. "The police and I go back a very long way. Before either one of you was even born. I understand them."

"And we understand you," Spaceman said.

"About Vacarro," Blue put in mildly.

"Yes, I heard he was dead. A street killing or some such thing, correct?"

"He was killed," Spaceman said savagely, "by the same person who's killed twice already this week."

Delvecchio smiled. "Crime in this city. Makes one think that the police should be out tracking down all these killers, instead of bothering old men."

Blue looked at Spaceman.

Spaceman looked at him, then at Delvecchio. "The name Hua mean anything to you?"

"Not a thing."

"Marybeth Wexler?"

"No."

"Wolf?"

"Three strikes, Detective Kowalski. And you are out."

Spaceman looked for someplace to extinguish his cigarette, finally crushing it out on the bottom of his shoe, and tucking the butt into the watch pocket on his jeans. "Although I admire you for trying, Papa, you really can't pull this off."

"What?"

"This act. The poor, helpless old man who doesn't know shit about drugs or murder or anything else. It just won't wash."

Delvecchio just smiled.

As if by magic, the maid reappeared. "This way out," she said.

Spaceman nodded. "Have a merry Christmas, Papa. We'll be in touch."

The only response was the return of the soap opera.

26

Lars searched for a match, finally found a battered book in his back pocket, lit one, and then struggled to keep the weak flame going against the brisk wind racing in off the Pacific. At this time of the night, in December, the beach could be a chilly, damp place to stand.

It certainly hadn't been his choice of a meeting place, especially at this hour, but then no one had asked his opinion of the arrangements; they just told him where and when. So here he was.

Not for the first time during the evening, he wished that either Dev or Toby had answered his repeated phone calls. It pissed him off a little that both of the creeps were out doing something else just when he needed them. Toby never even answered the messages left on his fucking machine. The two of them would have to be made aware that it was their duty to be available whenever necessary. Being AWOL was a capital offense, in case those two idiots had forgotten. Dealing with civilians was a pain.

And frankly, it made Lars nervous to be standing out here all alone. Somebody should be covering him. But nobody was. He sucked smoke into his lungs almost desperately.

"You Wolf?" The voice came from behind him suddenly.

Lars swore to himself. That was twice somebody had managed to get so close without his knowing. *I must be* slipping, he thought. "Yeah, I'm Wolf," he said tentatively. He figured it would be a wise move not to turn around.

"We understand that you are claiming an interest in certain items of value."

"Yeah," he said again. He dropped the cigarette and very carefully crushed it out in the damp sand. As he was doing that, his mind was quickly trying to hear something familiar in the voice. The man spoke with the careful precision of someone for whom English was not the first language, but beyond that Lars could tell nothing.

"The people I represent also have an interest in these items," the voice said.

"Is that so? Good for you."

A soft chuckle. "Our claim is better than yours, however. How do you Americans say it? Possession is ninety percent of the law?"

"Nine tenths. Possession is nine tenths of the law." Fucking foreigners, Lars thought. He turned his collar up against the wind. "So are you saying that the people you represent already have the stones?" God, they couldn't, not yet.

"In a manner of speaking."

Which meant, he decided, that they did not. A little of the tension left his body. "So what do you want with me then?"

There was a pause which went on so long that he thought the owner of the soft, sneaky voice had gone. But finally he spoke again. "That is the point, in fact."

"What is the point?"

"We want nothing at all to do with you. We want this annoying little insect who calls himself Wolf to stop bothering us. Otherwise, we might have to swat him."

"People keep telling me that," Lars said. "First the dagos and now you."

"Perhaps a wise man would begin to heed so much advice."

"Not possible," Lars said flatly.

Before there was any response, the silence of the beach was broken abruptly by the roar of a noisy old car somewhere very nearby. The area was swept by the glare of headlights that vanished as suddenly as they had appeared.

Lars waited, but nobody said anything, and finally he realized that this time the man was really gone. He turned. There was nobody on the long stretch of beach except for him and the dark shape of a car that probably held a couple of turned-on kids looking for a place to screw. "Shit," he said into the wind. Another waste of time. He was getting tired of fucking around with these people.

He trudged back to the road where his car was parked. What he needed was a better night's sleep than he would get in the backseat of this thing. Maybe a motel, although he was running a little short of ready cash. He kept meaning to make a run past the safety deposit box and get some.

Maybe he was too busy thinking about the logistics of it all, or maybe he was just too cold and tired and disgusted with life in general, but he never heard or suspected a thing until it was too late. For the third time lately.

The first blow came from nowhere, crashing across his back and knocking him to the ground. It was followed up by at least two sets of fists and booted feet working their way over his body.

Pretending not to struggle against what was happening, Lars curled as tightly as he could into a ball, trying to protect his head. At the same time, he reached inside the jacket and slid the gun out. He shoved the barrel into some flesh and fired.

Someone screamed, swore in Vietnamese, and rolled away from him. The creep wasn't dead, but he was hurting. Lars raised the gun again, but the two figures were already heading toward a van parked down the road. He fired once anyway, just to make sure they kept moving.

Then he passed out.

He had no idea how much later it was when he finally made his way back to the world of the living. At first, it seemed like the wrong thing to do. But staying where he was didn't seem like such a good idea either.

Lars had been through this kind of thing before, more often than he liked to remember, and the routine was automatic by now. He mentally checked over each part of his battered body, relaxing a little as he realized that nothing seemed to be broken.

The time he'd spent lying on the cold damp ground caught up with him, however, and he sneezed. The impact of that minor explosion nearly finished him off. Done in by a fucking sneeze, he thought wearily. Christ. He groaned into the chilly air and sat up. Each movement caused pain in some different place on his body. He rattled off profanities in several languages, including two obscure African dialects. That made him feel a little better.

He reached for the door handle and pulled himself up and then into the car. Once there and once his head had stopped pounding quite so hard, he checked his pockets, only mildly surprised to find that his wallet and gun were still in place. Which just proved what he already knew—that what had happened was no ordinary mugging and that the people behind it didn't want it mistaken as such. The beating was just supposed to strengthen the warning given by the soft-voiced stranger.

Fuck 'em.

He realized belatedly that blood was streaming from his nose. He tried rather uselessly to stanch the flow with his sleeve. "Shit," he said in a muffled voice. If ever, since the age of six or so, he'd felt the urge to cry, it would have been now. Not so much because he ached all over; he did, but he'd been hurt worse. It was just all so damned aggravating. And it was late and he was tired.

He started the car.

The pool and patio area of the Wilshire apartment complex were deserted, of course, as Lars made his way past them, trying to find apartment 12. He could only hope to hell that Dev was home; but then where else would he be at this hour?

He found 12, tucked away in the far corner of the apartment complex, and knocked, gently at first, then more firmly. It seemed to take a very long time before the door opened.

Devlin just stared.

Lars propped himself up against the door frame, trying to smile through swollen, bleeding lips. "Got a drink? I could sure as hell use a drink, mate."

"You could use a bloody doctor, you ass."

But Lars shook his head. Then he sneezed again, grabbing at his sore ribs. "Damn," he gasped. "That smarts, you know?" Then he looked at Devlin. "You gonna let me in or shall I just die right here on your doorstep?"

"Hell." Devlin helped him across the threshold and over to the couch, carefully lowering him onto the cushions, ignoring the mess of sand and blood. "What the devil happened?"

"Nothing I shouldn't have expected. Somebody doesn't want us to have our diamonds, lover, that's all. They think something like this will scare us off."

Devlin frowned. "Not a bad guess on their part. I'm beginning to wonder if this is such a good idea."

Lars just shrugged. "Get a towel or something, willya? Before I bleed all over the fucking place. And that drink?"

Devlin went into the other room and in a moment, Lars could hear water running. He leaned back gingerly and relaxed. This was a safe place, a place where he could ease up a little and let somebody else worry.

He closed his eyes.

27

The newsstand was on Third Street. Evening rush hour was just ending as Blue pulled the Porsche next to the curb and Spaceman signaled out the window with one hand.

The middle-aged proprietor brought a copy of the *Times* over to him. "You don't come around in a long time, Detective," he said.

"Been busy, Quoc." Spaceman took the paper and without looking tossed it toward Blue, who caught it just before it hit him in the nose. "What's going on these days?"

The moon-face creased in a bland smile. "What could I know?"

"Come off it, Quoc. Once a cop always a cop." He glanced at Blue. "My old friend here was a very big deal in the Saigon police department."

"A long time ago," Quoc demurred. But he straightened a little and smoothed the front of his gaudy cotton shirt.

"We're interested in who's doing what to who in your little corner of the world. And don't try to play dumb with me."

"Would I do that to a colleague?"

Spaceman just smiled noncommittally.

Quoc leaned against the car confidentially. "If I was in the market for information about current events, I would talk to Lin Pak."

"Pak? Who is that?"

"A greedy little man who likes to know where all the

corpses are buried. He deals in data. Facts for sale to the highest bidder. Pak and I are long-time acquaintances. Sometimes I used his talents in the old days. Sometimes I arrested him."

"Where can we find him?"

Quoc shook his head. "Men like Pak don't stay in one place very long. They cannot afford to. Ask around, is all I can say."

Spaceman realized that they wouldn't get anything more out of Quoc. He handed him a five to pay for the newspaper and signaled Blue to drive on.

They took the news vendor's advice and asked around a little, but there was no sign of Pak. It was time to call this day done.

On his way home, Blue stopped by Saks to pick up a new suit that had been altered to fit. While in the store, he bought a shirt and tie to go with the suit. Christmas presents for himself, he decided. After leaving Saks, he wandered into Van Cleef and Arpels and ended up with a gold and black sapphire ring as well. Why not? It was the only Christmas shopping he'd done, except for a bracelet he'd already given to Sharon and a bottle of ten-year-old Laphroaig whiskey for Spaceman.

Blue told himself, as the salesman wrote up the charge on the ring, that he wasn't buying it just because Sharon and the damned bracelet were already across the country. What the hell; he could afford the fucking ring and whatever else he wanted, so why shouldn't he have the things that made him happy?

What wouldn't make him happy, he decided, was going home and fixing dinner. Alone. So, instead, he stopped at La Scala Boutique for shrimp marinara and a pitcher of the house wine.

Conscientiously, he drank several cups of strong black coffee before leaving the restaurant.

It was after eleven by the time he finally pulled into the driveway and parked. The telephone was ringing as he unlocked the front door and he ran into the living room to answer it, almost tripping over the damned cat on the way.

"Where the hell have you been?"

The owner of the voice was drunker than he had been during any of the other calls.

Blue dropped the boxes and sat on the floor. "Who is this?" he asked, abruptly irritated by these continuing, mysterious intrusions into his life. Enough was fucking enough.

There was a long silence on the line.

"You mad, Loot? Hey, Maguire, you pissed at me?"

There was something so pathetic in the words that Blue was angry at himself for reacting the way he had. "No, I'm not mad." He leaned against the sofa, stretching his legs across the floor. "I'd just like to know who it is I'm talking to."

"I sorta thought you'd have it figured out by this time. You're supposed to be a cop, right?"

"I'm supposed to be. But maybe I'm just not very good at my job."

"No?"

"Maybe." He thought about the damned case. This should be his big chance; after all, he was the one who'd talked to Wexler. But what was he doing besides spinning his wheels?

The voice laughed. "Shit. Have you really been trying to find out who I am?"

"No."

"Why not?"

"No reason, really,"

"Didn't think it mattered much, right?"

"Maybe I just thought that you'd tell me, sooner or later." Blue pulled the boxes closer.

"No ideas at all?"

"Yes. I know that we spent time in the Hanoi Hilton together."

"Very good. See, you ain't such a bad cop."

"Tell me your name, please."

"It don't matter." There was no hint of either anger or hostility in the words, just a sort of weary emptiness that bothered Blue more than either of those emotions would have.

"It matters to me." He opened the smallest box and took out the ring.

"Why should it?"

"Maybe it shouldn't, but it does." He slipped the ring on, admiring the way it caught the light.

"Loot, it's time you faced the truth. I don't matter. You don't matter. None of it matters."

"Don't say that."

"Hey, buddy, if I can't tell you what I think, who can I tell? I can't afford no fucking shrink."

Blue shook his head.

"I'm scared, Maguire. More scared than I ever was back then. They're gonna get me one of these nights."

"Who?"

"You know."

"No, I don't. Tell me what's wrong and maybe I can help."

He laughed. "Oh, you stupid shit. How can you help me, Loot, when you can't even help yourself?"

For the first time, the caller hung up first.

Blue sat where he was, staring out over the city and occasionally reaching down to polish the new ring on the edge of his tie.

28

Toby turned off the tap, just as the hot, scented water reached the ultimate point, the level that would allow him to slip into the tub without flooding the floor of the hotel bathroom.

The woman stood in the doorway watching.

This was the way she liked to play the game. When he was in the tub, she would come into the room, kneel, and very carefully wash him. When the languid bath was over, he would get out of the tub and screw her right there on the carpeted floor of the steamy room. Frankly, he thought it was a little kinky, but she was paying and so she could do whatever turned her on.

Once he had finished with her, he was supposed to go back into the bedroom, take the money from the top of the dresser, get into his clothes quickly, and leave. When she wasn't horny anymore, she didn't want to see Toby Reardon.

Toby went through the motions perfectly, but more and more he found himself thinking about the day very soon when he wouldn't have to do this anymore. When he could fuck just for the fun of it.

Which was another thing. Toby was, honestly, getting tired of sex and he wasn't altogether sure that he would want to screw if it weren't strictly necessary. It was like a kid being paid to eat chocolate bars and, after so long a time, if somebody wasn't holding out the cash, he couldn't stand the taste.

What the hell. It didn't really matter. Toby thought that maybe he'd just take his million bucks and his boat and go off someplace all by himself. Except maybe he'd buy a dog. Something ugly and lovable.

He realized that time was moving and the broad in the can was starting to make getting up noises. Since he wasn't any more eager to see her than she was to encounter him, he quickly zipped the blue wool slacks, pulled the V-neck sweater on, and slipped into the loafers. Without even taking the time to comb his hair, he grabbed the money and ran.

Toby saw Lars before the other man spotted him. He was sitting in the hotel lobby bar, drinking a beer and eating pretzels from a wicker basket on the table.

Wistfully, Toby thought about slipping out the side door before Lars could see him. But that would only delay the inevitable.

So he walked over to the bar and dropped into the chair opposite Lars. It was only then that he noticed what a wreck Morgan was. Black eye, swollen lip, red nose. "Question number one," Toby said, "is how the hell do you keep finding me?"

Lars gave him a crooked, pained smile. "Secret of the trade, Tobias."

"Question number two: What the devil happened to you?"

Lars sneezed and used a paper napkin to wipe his nose. "I have a cold."

"Well, that explains it. Colds always give you a black eye, do they?"

He shrugged. "A slight altercation. Nothing to worry about."

"I stopped worrying about you years ago."

Lars gave him a dirty look, then said, "What you drinking?"

Thinking about all the cold germs floating around the table, Toby ordered a screwdriver, hoping that the oj would protect him. He picked up a pretzel and nibbled at the salt. The pretzel itself was stale. "I assume there was a reason for this meeting?"

"Yeah, I have an errand for you to run."

"What kind of an errand?" Toby asked suspiciously; he knew from long practice never to take anything Lars said completely at face value. Errand was a simple enough word, but there could be implications. With Lars, in fact, there usually were.

"A simple little errand is all."

The screwdriver arrived, along with another beer for Lars. Toby played absently with another pretzel. "Okay. Simple. What exactly?"

"I need you should go out to Pasadena and meet with a guy. He's supposed to have an envelope for me."

"What's in the envelope, Lars?" Toby asked gently.

"Christ, I'm a sick man and you want all the fucking details," Lars complained.

Toby smiled. "Hey, man, you'd lose all respect for me if I jumped into a hole without knowing what shit I'd find."

Lars sipped the beer, seeming to slosh the cool liquid around his sore mouth a little before swallowing. "I don't know exactly what will be in the damned envelope," he admitted reluctantly. "Hopefully, though, it will be the dope we need on when and where the diamonds are getting here."

"Okay. So why don't you go?"

He touched his face. "I'm a little too well-known lately. What's needed here is an unknown quantity."

After thinking about it for a moment, Toby nodded. "You know, though," he said, "this will fuck up my perfect record."

"What perfect record?"

"I've lived in Los Angeles for almost ten years and I've never been to Pasadena."

He pulled the modified VW, with its Rolls-Royce front end, to the curb and stared at the house. There was a for sale sign in the nearly grassless front yard and the windows were shuttered. Toby checked the address he'd scribbled on the matchbook cover. This was the place, all right. Before getting out of the car, he took one match and lit it, then ignited the rest of the book and dropped it into the ashtray, as Lars had ordered him to do.

The action amused him and he was still smiling as he approached the front door. Fun and games.

The whole block seemed deserted. Eerie kind of neighborhood. He knocked at the door, but no one opened it or even yelled for him to come on in. He took a chance and turned the knob. Unfortunately, the door opened. He'd been hoping to hell that it wouldn't, so he could go back to Lars and say he'd tried, but no luck.

He stepped inside. "Hello?" His voice echoed hollowly in the empty room. Against his better judgment, he walked through the living room, thinking that in a television cop show there would be body sprawled in the middle of the room.

He walked into the kitchen and the body was there.

There was a lot of blood puddled on the linoleum floor. Toby walked closer until he was staring directly down at the dead man. He looked with strange detachment at the ornate carved handle of the dagger piercing the corpse's chest.

A thought came that amused him again: At least Lars didn't shoot this one.

The amusement didn't last long. A faint sound that had been buzzing inside his head for several seconds finally became clear. It was a siren. A goddamned siren and it was coming closer. Cops. Cops, and here he was standing over the body of a murdered man.

Shit.

Toby turned on his heels and ran out of the house. He headed across the yard, reaching his car at the same moment that a squad car jackknifed to a stop. Two cops jumped out and they were both pointing guns at him.

"Freeze!" one cop yelled in his best Kojak manner.

Toby stopped so quickly that he slipped on the damp ground and fell forward, landing in the mud.

Damn Lars Morgan, he thought furiously, damn that bastard.

Then he put that aside, because there was no sense belaboring the obvious. He also didn't bother regretting the fact that he'd broken his record and come to Pasadena after all these years, just in time to be busted.

Instead, with his face pressed into the frigging mud, he tried to figure out how the hell he was going to save his ass.

29

His mood was improving. At first, when they'd hit Pasadena only to find the man they were looking for dead, Spaceman got pretty grouchy. But when he found out the local cops had a suspect, although not one they were too sure of, and that they would be more than happy to have Kowalski rake him over the coals a little, he cheered up some. Now he leaned way back in the chair and stared across the table. He'd never admit it, but this was kind of fun. The chance to play hardassed cop didn't come along so often these days. A small smile touched the corners of his mouth.

He was playing the game not only for the obvious audience, the suspect, but also for the Pasadena dick and Maguire, who were watching through the trick mirror and listening on the box.

Spaceman decided that the alleged perp was a pretty icy customer. He lounged in the straight-back chair easily, tanned and dressed in clothes that looked good even muddy. Not off the rack in Sears, for sure. He didn't even seem unduly fazed by being hauled in for questioning on a homicide.

Spaceman smiled more broadly. It was an expression peculiarly devoid of either humor or friendliness. "You wanna lose the shades, Reardon?" he said.

Reardon took off the mirrored glasses. " 'I trow that coun-

tenance cannot lie, whose thoughts are legible in the eye,' "
he said softly.

"What?"

"Matthew Roydon, 1593."

"Big deal." Spaceman glanced down at the paper in front
of him. "Reardon, Tobias James," he read aloud. "Age thirty-
six. Occupation . . . . occupation?" He looked up. "No visible
means of support?"

"I support myself. Very nicely in fact." He smiled brightly.

Spaceman was starting to get surly; smart asses like this
guy rubbed him the wrong way. "So how do you earn all
that money?"

Reardon pretended to think about it, shifting in the chair
and taking a moment to flash the grin into the mirror. He
apparently didn't want anybody thinking that they had him
fooled. Or maybe he just like looking at himself. Then his
attention returned to Spaceman. "I'm an escort," he said. "A
companion for the lonely. A professional gentleman."

Spaceman nodded. He took out his Bic and carefully
printed in the word *hustler* in large black letters on the line
provided. "I just like to have a complete picture of all my
suspects," he explained genially.

Reardon didn't say anything.

"Unless you object to that word?"

Reardon smiled again and shook his head.

"So. To business. You want to talk to me about Pak?"

"Who?"

"Pak. The deceased. The dead man you were running
away from when they nabbed you."

"Excuse me, Detective Kowalski, but did you ever stop to
think that maybe I was running to try and get some help for
the poor bastard?"

"Were you?"

"No." The single word was said with sudden and naked
honesty. "I was running away."

"Well, then?"

Reardon leaned forward a little. "Well, then nothing. I

mean, what would most people do if they walked in some-place and saw a body like that? I bet most others would run away, too."

"Maybe. But all those other folks weren't there. You were."

"I can explain that."

The smooth bastard could probably explain away every-thing from the Chicago fire to Richard Nixon, Spaceman thought sourly. "I'm listening."

Before Reardon could begin, the door opened and Blue came in. He sat in a chair by the door, not saying anything. Reardon just glanced at him. "Okay, I was driving by and I saw the for sale sign in the yard. It looked like a pretty nice place, so I stopped for a better look."

Spaceman sneered. "You thinking of setting up house-keeping, are you?"

"Why not? Everybody needs a home. I'm entitled, no matter what you might think of how I make my money."

Blue stirred. "So you stopped to look at the house. What happened then?"

"I knocked. But nobody answered, which didn't surprise me, because the place looked empty." He paused, brushing at some of the dried mud on his pants. "So I turned the knob. What the hell, right? And when the door opened, I went in. Just to get a good look, you know? But I sure wasn't expecting to see anything like that. Christ, I nearly puked. I mean, that guy was skewered."

Spaceman didn't much like this story; he also didn't like somebody wasting a man he was on his way to see. "You're telling us that you didn't know Pak at all?"

"I did not."

Spaceman tapped his fingers against the top of the table impatiently. "You know a man named Hua?"

"Hua?" After a pause, Reardon shook his head.

"You hesitated."

"Hell, man, I've met a lot of people. I had to think."

"How about Marybeth Wexler?" Blue asked.

"Huh-uh."

"Teddy Vacarro?" Spaceman said.

Reardon look annoyed. "Are you planning on working your way through the whole fucking telephone directory? Sooner or later you're bound to hit on somebody I know."

Blue scooted his chair a little closer. "Take it easy, Toby. One more name. Wolf. You know anybody who calls himself Wolf?"

"No."

"You didn't stop to think about it that time. Why?"

Reardon only shrugged.

The three of them sat looking at each other for a full two minutes. Then Spaceman hit the table with his hand. "To hell with it. The Pasadena dicks don't want you. And you're sure as hell not doing us any good. The prints on the knife weren't yours. Get the hell out of here."

Reardon unhurriedly got to his feet.

Blue grinned up at him. "You'll be around town, I expect, Mr. Reardon?"

"Where would I go? My business is here." He nodded pleasantly and left them alone in the interrogation room.

Spaceman said a dirty word.

30

Lars stared at his battered face in the mirror. Real terrific. He poked three more cold capsules out of the damned plastic wrapping and swallowed them all at once, not even bothering to wash them down with water.

He sneezed.

There was a loud knock on the motel room door and after one more grimace at his reflection, Lars hurried to answer it. "Where the hell have you been?" he said grouchily. "I expected you back hours ago."

Toby didn't answer. Instead, he pushed by Lars and stalked across the room to the bureau, which had been turned into a makeshift bar. He poured a healthy slug of vodka into a plastic cup, then downed it in one gulp. His stony gaze focused on Lars. "You bastard."

Lars was startled by the cold hatred in the other man's voice. "What?"

"Did you set me up?"

He was genuinely bewildered, both by the question and by the terrible ferocity of the man asking it. He took a good look at Toby, the muddy clotnes and five o'clock shadow. "What the fuck are you talking about?"

"That guy was dead when I got there."

"Pak?"

"Yes, Pak, yes. And right on cue, the pigs show up to find—surprise—Toby Reardon splitting the scene. I just love

137

it." He poured more vodka, but sipped it this time, still staring at him.

"You think it was a setup? That I set you up?"

"The thought had crossed my mind."

Lars shook his head. "Shit. I mean, shit, Tobias. I thought we were friends, for Chrissake. What kind of two-faced bastard do you think I am?"

"Maybe I don't know that as well as I thought I did. What kind of bastard are you, anyway?"

Lars didn't allow himself to get mad. "Okay, Tobias. Listen, just for the record, I did not set you up. Why the hell would I do something like that? We needed what Pak had. I need you." He sneezed three times in rapid succession, then wiped his nose on a Kleenex. "We're friends, damnit."

"Okay."

"Okay? That's all?"

Toby shrugged.

Lars shook his head. "I don't suppose Pak still had anything by the time you got there?"

"All I saw was the very long knife he had sticking in his chest." Toby drank again.

"That fucks us pretty good."

"Well, it almost got me permanently fucked."

"Yeah. Sorry about that."

Toby sat on the bed suddenly, as if very tired. "Prison life wouldn't suit me," he said in a slightly shaky voice.

"Don't worry about it. I take care of my men, right?"

"Right, yeah."

"You didn't tell the cops anything, did you?"

"Of course not. I made out like an innocent passerby. But I'm not sure they bought it." He sipped vodka. "They threw some names at me."

"Names?"

"Hua. Some broad. That dago you blew away. What's that all about?"

"Nothing important." Lars paced the room.

"They also asked me if I knew anybody named Wolf."

He stopped. "They did? Damn the bitch." His head was beginning to pound again. "Tobias, never trust a woman."

"I never would. So what happens next?"

"More work. I have to track down an alternate connection. Don't worry about it; I'm covered. We're covered. It's just that time is running out so damned fast." He walked over to the bar and poured himself a drink. "To success," he toasted.

Toby nodded. "And by the way," he said. "I'm sorry."

"For what?"

"Thinking that you set me up."

"I don't treat my friends that way."

"Okay, okay. I was just ticked off." He smiled. "You have a lot of friends, do you, Wolf?"

Lars sat on the other end of the bed and swallowed whiskey. "Well, counting you, which I'm not so sure is a good idea, and counting Dev, the final number comes to about two."

Toby snickered.

Lars stared at him. "And what about you, Tobias?"

After a moment, he shrugged and changed the subject.

31

"It's Christmas Eve, you know. Some of us have things to do." Spaceman had been bitching for an hour, ready to leave the office.

Blue didn't even bother to look up from the report he was reading. "So go," he said. "Nobody has you cuffed to the damned chair."

But Spaceman didn't get up. He had one foot propped against the desk and he used it to swivel his chair back and forth slowly. "What about you?"

"I'm waiting for a call."

Spaceman didn't say anything.

Finally Blue closed the file. "I asked Randolph to do some more checking on that guy Reardon. Maybe he'll get back to me with something."

"Tonight? I doubt it. And whatever he might get will still be here after Christmas."

"Look, Lainie is waiting for you. Go."

Instead, Spaceman lit a cigarette. "You still getting those phone calls?"

Blue shrugged. "Sometimes."

"Any idea yet who it is?"

"I'm working on it." The tone was dismissive.

"Be careful," Spaceman said flatly.

After a moment, Blue nodded.

The phone rang shrilly and he grabbed it. "Maguire here.

Yeah, Randolph, what'd you get?" He listened for a moment, frowning. "Okay, you'll keep on it? Thanks. Yeah, same to you." He hung up.

"Well?"

"He couldn't get any details, because of the damned holiday, but he did find out one interesting fact."

"Which is?"

"That Reardon was in Nam. In the Special Forces."

Spaceman lowered his foot to the floor. "Just like Wolf in the picture, right?"

"Right."

"Well, I guess that doesn't have to mean anything. Necessarily."

Blue nodded. "Necessarily. It probably doesn't mean shit, in fact. But still, it's interesting. We might want to keep an eye on good old Toby."

"Yep, I think so." Spaceman stood. "Come on, it's time to get the hell out of here."

Blue shrugged. "Guess so."

They walked out of the building without talking and crossed the lot to where their respective cars were parked side by side. There, they both hesitated.

"So," Spaceman said. "Have a good Christmas."

"Sure, you too. Give Lainie my best."

Spaceman nodded. They got into their cars, then he rolled down the window. "You've got plans, right?"

Blue smiled and waved as he drove away.

32

The bar was crowded and noisy, jammed mostly with people who didn't have anyplace else to spend this night or anybody better than a bunch of strangers to spend it with. Most of the fevered celebrants would probably have preferred to be somewhere other than the Galaxy Lounge, but they were all making the best of it.

Lars Morgan, however, wasn't pretending to enjoy himself; he really was having a good time. Even the lingering effects of the beating and his cold couldn't dent his spirits. "You know, Dev," he said, "this is the first Christmas we've spent together in about eight years."

Devlin just nodded.

Lars peered at him. "You down about something?"

Now he smiled faintly. "Just a case of nerves, I guess."

"Hell, there's nothing to be nervous about. I've got everything under control."

"I was talking about the opening of my show, you idiot. The bloody diamonds are your problem."

"No problems at all tonight, lover." Lars reached into his pocket and pulled out a quarter. "Call it," he said, tossing the coin.

"Heads."

He grinned. "Sorry."

Devlin shrugged. "You're on a roll, Morgan. Go for it." He still didn't sound very enthusiastic.

Lars frowned. "You really want to play the game, Dev?"

He smiled again. "Sure. Of course, Lars. Pick a winner."

Lars got up and began a slow walk around the room. He wanted to find a special broad for tonight. It was Christmas, after all, and this choice would be sort of like a present to Dev. Knowing just what kind of woman most appealed to his friend, Lars passed up several possibilities, finally settling on a tall, willowy blond at the bar. She didn't look like the kind of woman who would be hustling in a bar, but he supposed that was just a matter of degree. A whore was a whore, whether she stood out on Hollywood Boulevard or whether she worked out of a fancy Beverly Hills apartment by "referral only."

He stopped next to her. "Hi."

"Hello," she said in a voice that was soft and sexy as velvet.

Lars rested one arm across the back of her stool. "We could waste a lot of time here," he said. "But why bother?"

"Time is money," she said.

"Right. I have a friend over there, the good-looking Aussie. He and I would like you to spend some time with us this evening. If you know someplace close by."

"As it happens, I do." She looked him up and down speculatively, then glanced toward Dev. "You're not cops I hope?"

He grinned and shook his head.

"Two on one?"

"Nope. Just one and then the other."

"Time and half, since it's a holiday."

He shrugged. "What the hell."

She picked up her purse from the bar and slid from the stool.

Lars gave a quick thumbs-up gesture to Devlin, who signaled his approval.

Lars drank a beer as he undressed slowly. There were still

several good-sized bruises along his rib cage. The woman was already naked, sitting on the bed and smoking a pastel cigarette. Even without clothes she was a classy broad. Elegant.

Devlin seemed vaguely amused by the whole thing. He got like that sometimes. Lars often thought that Devlin didn't really believe anything was true unless he saw it through the camera lens. It could be he was right.

Lars grinned at Devlin, then slid into the bed next to the woman. She smelled of violets and something else, something heavy and musky.

Across the room, he could see the orange glow from Devlin's cigarette and hear the mild pop of another beer being opened. Someplace down the hall, a radio was playing Christmas carols.

Lars relaxed, allowing his control to loosen, so he was caught up in the smells and the feel of the woman's mouth on him and the throbbing music. The whore was good and when he finally crashed over the edge in climax, it left him exhausted and sweaty, breathing heavily.

Too tired even to walk across the room to the chair, he just rolled off the bed and rested there, leaning against the mattress. He felt the bed shift as Devlin got in. A hand reached down and placed a freshly lit cigarette between his lips. He inhaled gratefully.

Just at that moment, fleetingly, Lars felt that if something happened to screw everything up and they never got the damned diamonds, he could still be happy.

Blue parked the car. From where he was, he could see the boat that belonged to Toby Reardon. There was a light on in the cabin. Blue snapped the plastic lid off the coffee cup and sipped the cooling liquid.

He didn't really know what had possessed him to drive out to Marina del Rey just to sit and stare at Reardon's boat, but here he was. It was chilly down by the water.

The door to the cabin opened and Reardon appeared. Blue slid down in the seat, although there was no reason to think that Reardon would think he was being watched by the cops. Especially a cop in a Porsche.

Reardon was wearing a heavy sweater and drinking something from a white mug. He was alone. All he did was stand at the railing and stare out over the water. Hell of a way to spend Christmas Eve, Blue thought.

After thirty or so minutes, Reardon went back inside. Shortly, the light went off.

God rest ye merry, Blue thought sourly.

Cold and tired, he started the car and left.

33

Light and noise crashed in on him. He woke sharply, filled with terror. It took him an endless moment to remember that he was home, on the boat, and then more time to realize that he wasn't alone.

"Reardon?" The voice was rough as gravel and absolutely unfamiliar.

Blinking against the flashlight that was aimed directly at his face and trying not to shiver from the touch of deadly cold steel against his chest, Toby nodded.

"We want Wolf. You know where he is?"

"Maybe." The gun barrel jabbed into him. "Hey, take it easy. I'll tell you what I know. I know where he might be."

"Better than telling us, we'll all go there together."

He was nudged up from the bed. "Can I put some clothes on first?"

Suddenly, unexpectedly, the man laughed; it was an ugly sound. "Sure, sweetheart," he said, bringing one hand down to smack Toby's bare ass. "No sense causing fucking riots in the streets, right?"

Toby moved a couple of steps, fumbling in the early-morning half-light for a pair of jeans. "Why me?" he said.

"Hey, don't take it personal. Boss says visit Toby Reardon, we do."

"I'm nobody."

"Yeah, well, you're a nobody that's been hanging tight with Wolf."

"My mistake."

"Probably," the guy said cheerfully.

Toby pulled the white sweater on and slid his feet into the loafers. "My glasses," he said, running one hand through his hair. "I have to find my goddamned glasses." He spotted them on the table and put them on. The three men were all armed. Toby shook his head vaguely. "Hey, what the hell," he said suddenly. "Isn't this Christmas? Isn't this fucking Christmas Day?"

The leader grinned, showing a set of teeth badly in need of orthodontic work. "Season's greetings, sweetheart."

Toby directed them to the only place he could think of: Devlin Conway's apartment. He didn't honestly think they'd find Lars there, but he hoped and prayed that Conway would know where he was. Tight as they were, it made sense.

At a nod from the boss, Toby pounded on the door. He wondered what the neighbors would think, if anybody looked out and saw what looked like the cast from a bad gangster movie gathered.

It took a couple minutes of hard knocking before they heard a voice from inside. "Yeah? What the hell is going on?" The door swung open. Devlin, wearing only shorts and obviously just awake, stood there. "Toby, what the—" He saw the whole group and shut up abruptly.

"These, uh, gentlemen would like to see Wolf. I thought you might know where to find him."

Devlin stared at Toby for a moment, then glanced back into the living room.

"Let them in," Lars said.

They stepped inside and somebody closed the door. Lars had apparently been sleeping on the couch. He was wide awake now though, propped against one arm of the leather sofa, the blanket kicked aside and a gun in his hand. The gun was pointing toward them.

Steel rammed again into Toby's spinal column. He had a moment of panic, made worse when he saw Morgan's emotionless slate eyes. Don't point the fucking thing at me, he wanted to tell the creep holding the gun, Morgan doesn't give a damn. Point it at Conway; he won't let you shoot the Aussie.

But then Lars lowered his gun. "What's this all about?" he said reasonably enough.

Toby exhaled as the gun in his back was removed.

"Mr. Delvecchio would like to take a meeting with you, Wolf."

"It's Christmas."

"Yeah, that's what everybody keeps saying."

"Shit," Lars said mildly. But then he got up from the couch and reached for his shirt. He'd apparently been sleeping in jeans and socks. He buttoned the shirt slowly. "Just where are were going?"

"You'll know when we get there." The barrel of the gun touched lightly against Toby's spine again. "You come, too."

"Why me?" he said again.

"Why not?"

That seemed sufficient reason.

Devlin was leaning against the wall, still looking half asleep and bewildered. "What about me?" he said.

"Boss didn't say nothing about you. Must be your lucky day."

Lars finished dressing. "Well, let's go then, damnit." He glanced at Devlin. "See you later."

Devlin just nodded.

Inside one of the neighboring apartments somebody started playing the Johnny Mathis Christmas album. It was a nice touch.

Lars and Toby were jammed into the backseat with one of the armed gorillas, while the other two sat in the front.

Toby's mouth was so dry that he could hardly even swallow. Lars, on the other hand, seemed totally at ease, whistling "I'll Be Home For Christmas" under his breath and relaxing as best he could in the crowded seat.

Toby looked at him and Lars winked reassuringly.

Toby wasn't especially reassured.

The car finally stopped, someplace along the Santa Monica beach, and they all piled out. The ocean was choppy and there was a sharp breeze blowing across the sand. Probably later the day would be warm enough for all the transplanted Easterners to come down and go into the water, at least briefly. They could then let all the folks back home know that in the promised land you could actually swim on Christmas Day.

But right now, Toby was cold, even in the heavy sweater. He shoved both hands into the pockets of his jeans as they walked across the beach to where another car, this one a long black limo, was already parked. As they arrived, the back door opened and two men stepped out. One looked like a lawyer, three-piece suit, briefcase, and all. The other was too old by a couple of decades to be hanging around the beach at the frigging crack of dawn. He wore a heavy overcoat, though, so at least he was probably warm.

Maybe because it was so unpleasant on the beach or maybe because this was Christmas and everybody had better things to do, nobody wasted any time on the amenities.

"Wolf," the old man said, "You were warned to back away. Instead of taking this friendly advice, however, you killed my messenger."

"Vacarro pulled a gun on me," Lars said. "I thought he might use it. Whatever happened to him was strictly self-defense."

"That is maybe true, but it is not particularly relevant."

Delvecchio stared out across the grey water thoughtfully. "I don't have much time to spend on you. My grandkids are going to open their gifts very soon and I should be there. The family is important." He glanced at them again. "You know, Wolf, in the old days we wouldn't even be having this conversation, because you would already be dead. Things were easier then. Now . . . " He gestured toward the briefcase toter. "Now everything is lawyers and committees. Even a simple hit is a big deal."

Toby was trying not to listen, figuring that the less he knew, the better. An old man talking about killing him was not especially what he wanted to hear, anyway. He turned away from the conversation to watch the water, pretending that he was out there safely on his boat.

"Wolf, these diamonds you are chasing belong to me. Or I should be specific: They will be mine in a very short time. The deal has come down and there's no room for you and your associates."

Toby considered raising his hand and volunteering the information that at least one associate was quite willing to step out of the picture. Instead, he glanced at Lars.

The man he saw standing next to him was the Morgan he remembered from Nam. Tough, cold, unyielding. To hell with the fact that Lars was a little crazy; when things got rough, you wanted him there and in charge. "I think the stones rightfully belong to anyone who can get them, Papa D.," he said in a cold, even voice. "This is still the home of free enterprise, right? And our claim is older and better than yours."

He had a point, Toby thought, the bastard had a damned good point. There was a long silence, during which he watched two gulls fight over a fish.

"Even today there are limits, Wolf," Delvecchio said. "You have just reached yours. Any more trouble and it will be easier to kill you, even if it makes the lawyers frown."

The lawyer frowned.

"Understand?" the old man said. "There won't be any more warnings."

"Fine."

In another moment, Delvecchio and his legal beagle got back into the limo and drove off. The three apes climbed into their car and left, too. It got very quiet.

"How the fuck are we supposed to get home?" Toby said.

Lars shrugged. "Find a phone. Call Dev. He'll come get us."

"Great." They started walking. "Do you know what I was going to do this morning?"

Lars grunted in the negative as they trudged toward the highway.

"I was going to make a pitcher of Bloody Marys and stay in bed. Plug in the old Betamax and watch a Bogart film festival. It's what I do every Christmas."

"Yeah?" Lars lighted a cigarette, handed it to him, then lit another for himself.

Toby smoked in silence for a time. "Why didn't he just kill us?" he asked finally.

"Like he said. The lawyers don't like it."

"Yeah?" Toby said skeptically.

"Well, that's part of it. Maybe another part is that I hear a federal committee on organized crime is poking a little too close. Delvecchio is an old man. He wants to spend his last years in Palm Springs, not Leavenworth. So, if he can avoid stirring things up too much right now, he will."

"I guess that makes sense." Toby kicked at an empty Coke can. "So what happens next?"

"Nothing."

"Nothing?"

"I mean, nothing's different. We just keep at it." Lars glanced at him. "Or are you losing your taste for this little adventure, Tobias? It's harder than screwing old ladies for a buck, right?"

Toby got mad suddenly. "Fuck off, Morgan." He pointed

to a spot a hundred yards or so up the road. "A phone."

Lars laughed softly, although there was nothing funny. Maybe it was just the spirit of the season.

Toby threw the cigarette butt away. As far as he was concerned, to hell with the season, to hell with old men talking about death, and to hell with Lars Morgan.

34

Blue looked up and saw his partner approaching.

Ostentatiously, he glanced at his watch, which showed almost fifteen minutes past the time Spaceman should have arrived, but all he said was, "Love the tie."

Spaceman glanced down at the wide swath of purple and yellow stripes that adorned his chest. "Yeah?" he said doubtfully. "The kid gave it to me."

Blue personally thought that Robbie must have been joking, but he didn't say so.

Spaceman dropped heavily into his chair, smoothing the tie over the faded madras sport shirt he was wearing. "You know what my New Year's resolution is going to be?"

"What's that?"

"To drop ten pounds."

"Terrific," Blue said. "Why not go for fifteen?"

But Spaceman shook his head. "I don't want to get all gaunt looking. Besides, if I lost that much, none of my clothes would fit."

Which in Blue's eyes would have been an additional blessing. But discretion being the better part of a relationship, he did not say that. "Where the hell are we going with this thing?" he asked instead, indicating a pile of folders on the desk.

"Which particular thing is that?"

"Wolf, of course." As far as he was concerned, all their other cases were way back on the burner.

"Of course." Spaceman leaned back dangerously in his chair. "Ah, you know, I'm beginning to feel a sneaky fondness for that bastard. I mean, anybody who puts the screws to Papa D. can't be all bad."

Blue frowned and twisted a paper clip out of shape. "I'm glad you've found a new hero to admire. It's just a shame that we can't ask Marybeth Wexler what she thinks about him. Or Hua."

Spaceman acknowledged that with a shrug. "Has anything come back from Washington on the photo? Or the name Wolf?"

"No. I checked a couple times yesterday and first thing this morning."

"Yesterday?" Spaceman looked at him. "What the fuck were you doing in here yesterday?"

Blue regretted the slip. He shrugged.

"Working on Christmas, when we had the day off. Shit."

"I just caught up on some paperwork. Things were quiet."

"I can imagine."

Blue slammed the desk drawer closed. "I think everybody in the government went to Florida for the holidays."

"Probably. And probably at my expense. Well, we'll just have to muddle along without them, won't we, partner?"

"For as much good as it will do us," Blue said glumly.

As the day went on, his pessimism seemed more than justified. It was one of those shifts when absolutely nothing happened; a detective's nightmare that was all too common in real life. Hours of muddling along with names and rumors netted them a flat zero.

They had lunch at a Mexican joint on Alverado, where Spaceman knew everybody and Blue decided going in that he was going to get indigestion.

Over the tacos, Spaceman seemed lost in thought, which

suited his partner just fine. But then he looked up. "You should've called," he said suddenly.

"What?"

"Hell, we had plenty of food and stuff. You could've come out and had Christmas dinner with us."

Blue shrugged, finishing the last bite of his taco.

"You like being a fucking martyr?"

He smiled. "Next time, I'll call," he said.

"All right," Spaceman said, seemingly mollified.

Things got no better after lunch. By the time they signed out, neither detective had much holiday cheer left. The fact that there had been no new killings by Wolf was the only thing that even resembled a bright spot.

Without even discussing the matter, they both walked across the street to the Lock-up. In the bar, they isolated themselves in a rear booth and downed some beer, not talking.

After two drinks, Blue stood. "I'm going to a gallery opening," he said. "You want to come along?"

Spaceman was unwrapping a package of cheese crackers. He looked skeptical, then shook his head. "Maybe next time," he said. "Enjoy yourself."

The Addison Gallery was ablaze with lights when Blue pulled up and parked the Porsche. At the door, he displayed the opening night invitation and was waved in. Addison himself was nearby, greeting the arrivals. There was a respectable turnout, considering that it was still the holiday season and that the subject matter of the exhibit could hardly be called cheerful. That so many of the town's beautiful people had shown up was due, no doubt, to the influence of Addison himself. He was, in Blue's opinion, something of a fussy ass, but still a powerhouse on the local art scene.

He saw Blue and brightened. "Blue, so nice to see you. It's been too long." He probably was happy, considering just for example, the price Blue had paid for the Monet in his living room.

Blue replied with all the right words.

"I think you'll find this most interesting. Wander, look, have some refreshment. The photographer himself is here, too."

Blue nodded and moved off as Addison turned to welcome someone else. He picked up a glass from a passing tray and sipped the just barely adequate champagne as he started around the room.

He wasn't quite sure why he was here; the past was something he tried not to think about. Maybe it was because of the damned telephone calls; maybe he thought there could be some kind of answer in the pictures.

The images of war hit him harder than he had thought they would. He moved slowly, from picture to picture, separate from all the people around him, lost in memory.

"You were there, right?"

Blue, startled, glanced sidewise at the tall, dark-haired man next to him. Like Blue, he wore a white dinner jacket and held a glass of the pitiful champagne. "It shows?" Blue said ruefully.

"Yes. To the practiced eye. Something in the way you stand. Defensive. Or aggressive maybe. But it shows."

Blue heard the accent and remembered what he'd read in the catalogue. "You're Devlin Conway, right?"

"Guilty."

"Blue Maguire." They shook hands. "Your pictures are terrific."

"Thank you."

Blue sipped champagne and tried to put into words what he was feeling. "They're almost too real. I mean, photographs show reality, but these . . . they show the truth, too. If that makes any sense."

"It does."

Blue moved on a little and Conway moved with him. The stark black and white portrait of a naked child sitting on the ground next to his dead mother needed no comment. Blue just shook his head.

He stopped at the next picture. "God, this brings it all

back," he said in a voice that wasn't entirely steady. The sweaty, anguished face of a young soldier stared at him, so real that it almost seemed he would speak.

"Maybe we don't want it brought back." Conway said.

Blue shrugged. Abruptly, he leaned forward to get a better look. The face of the soldier was strangely familiar. Someone he had known over there? The eyes seemed to pierce him and suddenly Blue realized who the young man was. "Who is that?"

Conway didn't say anything.

Blue turned to look at him. "Do you know who this is?"

"Why?" Conway was watching the crowd.

"I have a good reason for asking," Blue said, trying to keep his voice calm. "I'm a detective with the L.A.P.D."

Now Conway shot him a quick look, then he glanced at the picture. "I don't know," he said flatly. "Why should I? I don't know who any of these subjects are. They were just there. And that was a long time ago."

Blue stared at him, wondering. Conway did not meet his gaze.

Conway finally gave him a weak smile. "Excuse me, but Addison is waving me over."

"Nice talking to you," Blue said absently.

Conway nodded and moved away quickly. Too quickly?

Blue turned back to the photograph once again. It was the man they knew as Wolf, no doubt about it. He took a deep breath. Damn. Damn.

Devlin unlocked the door and went into his apartment.

The only light in the living room came from the dim glow of the television screen. Lars, who was apparently here for the duration, was stretched out on the couch, a can of beer balanced on his stomach. His eyes were closed.

As Devlin ripped off the damned tie and jacket, he watched the even rise and fall of the other man's chest. Then he sat down on the edge of the couch and took the beer can.

Lars smiled without opening his eyes. "So, big shot, how'd it go?"

The beer was flat and warm, but Devlin drank some anyway, because his mouth was so dry. "There was a cop."

Lars scooted up a little and opened his eyes. "What?"

"There was cop at the show."

"Doing what?"

"Looking at the fucking pictures, Lars, what do you think?"

"So?"

Devlin tried to settle his jangled nerves. "So when he saw the picture of you, he asked me about it."

Lars was wide awake now. "What did he ask?"

"If I knew who the soldier was."

"And what did you say?" Lars asked in a gentle voice.

"I said no, of course."

Lars relaxed. "Okay, no problem."

"Why was he asking?"

"How the hell do I know?" Lars said irritably. "Probably just because that's what cops do. Ask questions. It makes them happy. Just don't worry about it. Things are happening very fast now. Couple more days at the most and we'll have our fucking stones, lover. The cops can play with themselves all they want then."

Devlin wanted to ask more about the cop and about just what was happening, but he knew the tight-jawed expression on Lars' face too well. The smartest thing he could do was shut up about that subject.

He took another sip of the warm beer and then he started talking again. But it wasn't about the cop or even the diamonds. Instead, he talked about the good things that had happened during the evening. The praise his photographs had received. The number of people who seemed keen to buy.

Lars stretched out again to listen, a faint smile on his face.

35

Spaceman was beginning to get a little nervous. On Christmas Eve, for the hundredth or so time, he'd asked Lainie to move in with him. Except that this time, instead of just making some kind of joke about it, she thought for a moment, then said that it might be a good idea.

But now he was getting itchy.

Not that he didn't want Lainie to live with him. He did. For sure. He thought.

The problem was, he hadn't lived with anybody since the end of his marriage, so his previous experience was less than terrific on any number of counts. He didn't want to fuck up what was now a perfectly good relationship.

As he turned into the parking lot, Spaceman was seriously considering asking his partner's advice on the matter. Which was, he realized with dismay, some comment on the desperation of the situation. Asking anybody for help didn't come easily to Kowalski, but anybody as smooth and classy as Maguire, with all that dough to boot, had to know the tricks of handling broads.

Not that Lainie was a broad. Far from it; she was a lady from the word go.

Spaceman almost wished he'd never met her, because it was all getting so complicated.

He was surprised to see Blue in the parking lot, sitting on

the front of the Porsche and looking impatient. He pulled in next to the green car and got out.

"You're late again," Blue said immediately.

He glanced at his Timex. "Four fucking minutes, for Chrissake. You gonna snitch to the captain?"

Blue slid from the car. "I've got something to show you."

"Okay, show me."

"Not here. Get in, I'll drive."

Spaceman glanced toward the station. "But—"

"I already signed us both in." Blue looked at him. "This really can't wait, Spaceman." He seemed to be practically jumping out of his skin with eagerness.

Spaceman gave up and got into the Porsche. He reached for a cigarette and it was immediately clear just how stirred up Blue was; there was no dirty look for smoking in his car. "So you wanna give me a hint about what's going on?"

Blue took a deep breath as he propelled the car through the morning traffic. "I went to that gallery opening last night, remember?"

"Yeah?"

"It was called Visions of Vietnam. Photographs, you know, taken by an Australian photographer named Devlin Conway."

"Uh-humm. Terrific. Except that I don't need any Instamatics of that pisshole, thank you very much."

"Actually, it was good. The pictures, I mean. Real stark and yet sort of dreamlike—"

"Blue," Spaceman interrupted warningly.

"What?" He glanced over, swerving to avoid a jogger at the same moment. "Oh, sorry."

"If I want artsy-fartsy, I'll read *Time* magazine. Just tell me what the hell is going on."

"There's a picture I want you to see. But don't make me say anymore about it now. Not until you've seen it."

Spaceman grunted and concentrated on finishing his cigarette.

The Addison Gallery was just opening as they arrived and no one was there except a very stacked blond receptionist. She dismissed Spaceman with a glance and gave Blue a long look, which he didn't even seem to notice. Shaking his head, Spaceman followed his partner.

"There," Blue said, pointing. "Look at that."

With an indulgent attitude, Spaceman looked. The picture of the soldier brought a rush of memories, but he pushed them aside, as he always did, concentrating instead on the face. "Wolf," he said almost instantly. "That's Wolf."

Blue exhaled, as if he'd been holding his breath a long time. "Yes," he said. "That's what I thought."

"I'll be goddamned."

"I asked Conway about the picture, but he claimed not to know who the guy is."

Spaceman didn't miss the choice of words. "Claimed not to know?" he said.

Blue let his gaze survey the walls, all the pictures. "Well, what he said made sense. That he couldn't possibly know who all these people were. Especially after all these years."

Spaceman agreed. "So?"

"But it was the way he said it," Blue insisted. "I don't know, Spaceman, but I just didn't buy it." He spoke firmly enough, but there was a shadow of indecision in his eyes.

Spaceman was quiet briefly, not wanting to blow this moment. It could sometimes be a handicap working with a partner who doubted his own capabilities. To be good at what they did required a certain amount of arrogance. Which Blue Maguire seemed not to have much of. "Shit, you may have something here, Blue," he said finally. Although the words were sincere, he said them with somewhat more heartiness than came naturally.

Blue relaxed visibly.

"Do we have anything on this Conway?"

"I only spoke to him for a couple of minutes. But I got his address from the receptionist here."

"Good." Spaceman looked over at the woman, who had

probably wanted to give Maguire a lot more than that. Then he glanced back at the picture. There was such a thing as luck in this business. But all the luck in the world wasn't worth a pail of warm piss without the instinct. That instinct was what he had and maybe Maguire had it, too.

It was beginning to look like Wolf didn't stand a chance.

36

Lars could feel a growing sense of excitement that was almost sexual. Although, in fact, this was better, because there was always another fuck down the road, but here was his chance to make the big score of all time, and how often did that happen to a man?

None of what he was feeling showed, either on his face or in the easy slouch of his body in the chair. He tilted the beer can up and took a long drink of breakfast.

Devlin appeared in the doorway. "Do you want me to come along?" he said. He hadn't shaved yet and his eyes were bloodshot from too much booze and not enough sleep the night before.

"Not necessary. Tobias and I can handle this just fine."

Devlin leaned against the wall. "Toby sounded a little pissed on the phone before."

Lars just smiled. "He'll settle down. Basically because, if somebody is going to get left behind on anything, he doesn't want it to be him. Tobias still doesn't quite trust me not to shaft him."

"Jackass."

"Ah, well, not everybody has your touching faith in me." He finished the beer and tossed the empty can at Devlin, who caught it backhanded. "I better get my ass in gear. Tran is nervous and I don't want him bolting on me."

Devlin crushed the can easily. "This thing is almost over, right?"

"Right, lover," Lars said, heading for the bathroom. "Almost over."

Lars—showered, shaved, and dressed—was waiting on the sidewalk when the silver VW pulled up less than thirty minutes later.

Behind the wheel, Toby looked sullen.

"Cheer up, buddy," Lars said as he got in. "Those diamonds are so close that I can almost smell them."

"Right. Well, I'm worried. The cops already talked to me and Devlin told me what happened at the opening last night."

"I told him not to worry about that."

"Fine. Maybe he isn't. I am."

Lars glanced at him, a small smile flickering across his face. "Lemme tell you something, babe."

"What?"

"If you're looking for something to worry about, I suggest you put the cops pretty far down on the list."

"Oh?" Toby shifted gears gratingly.

"You better believe it. All they can do is ask their stupid questions and maybe, just maybe, bust you. Papa D. can kill us. He's already promised that, right? And as for the gooks, I wouldn't even like to think about what they might do."

Toby sighed. "Thanks. You're very comforting, you bastard."

Lars just shrugged.

Tran sat near the back of the run-down diner, nervously drinking coffee from a chipped mug. He barely looked up when they sat down across from him.

Lars signaled the fat waitress for two more cups. She

waddled over with them, poured some pale brown liquid into both, and left. "Well?" Lars said then.

Tran dabbed at his mouth with a crumpled paper napkin. "My father always said that you Americans were nothing but a bunch of wild cowboys."

"Did he? Gosh, that's really interesting," Lars said, dumping too much sugar into his cup. The words dripped with sarcasm.

Toby sipped his coffee as if he didn't quite trust it.

"Phillipe, you want to know something?"

"What?"

"I don't give one good flying fuck what your father used to say, okay?"

"There is a point to what I said."

"Oh, wonderful." He nudged Toby with an elbow. "Phillipe here has a point. What is it?"

Rather surprisingly, Tran smiled. "If you keep on doing what you are doing, you will probably die." It was just a fact the way he said it, not a threat.

Lars pushed at his hair absently. "Well, I look at it like this, Phillipe. Whatever I do or don't do about the stones, I'm going to be dead. Sooner or later."

"In this kind of trouble, I think sooner, much sooner," Tran said. He looked at Toby. "Wolf here talks big, like always. But maybe you don't feel the same. Maybe you're not a cowboy."

Toby was quiet, then he shrugged. "I'm in this with Lars," he said. "Wherever it goes. Whatever. I'll be dead one day, too."

"Thank you," Lars said, his voice only slightly mocking.

"Shit. Everybody ought to be a cowboy once in a while." Toby smiled sheepishly. "Actually, I wasn't quite sure until this moment. But it's true." He nodded. "I'm in till the end."

Lars turned his attention back to Tran. "See? Now tell us what we want to know."

Tran shook his head, apparently giving up. "The diamonds are arriving Wednesday night."

"Where?"

He took a slip of paper from his pocket and slid it across the table toward them. "Everything I could find out is written down here." He didn't let go of the paper yet. "When do I get my ten grand?"

Lars gently forced the paper from beneath the other man's fingers. "When I have the stones. We'll be in touch then. Earlier if we need you. Take off."

Tran hesitated, then left the diner in a hurry.

Lars watched the door swing closed after him. "I don't trust that little prick," he muttered.

"Hell, he's just hustling for his cut. Like the rest of us."

"Well, he better play it straight with me."

Toby smiled. "Who the hell would dare cross you?"

"Nobody more than once." Lars threw a couple coins down onto the table. "Come on, let's get out of this joint. There's a lot to do between now and Wednesday."

He was still excited and feeling good. Things were rolling, damnit, and this time they were rolling his way.

37

"This really bothers me," Blue said as they checked the row of mailboxes.

"Why?" Spaceman pointed at a box with the neatly typed name Conway above it.

"Conway is an artist with the damned camera. I mean, you saw those pictures. Why the devil would he be mixed up in whatever the hell is going on here?"

"We don't know that he is mixed up in anything," Spaceman said reasonably.

Blue wasn't in the mood for reason. "I've got a bad feeling about it," he muttered.

Hell, you gave a guy credit for a little instinct and he immediately went all weird on you. Feelings and vibes. Wonderful. Spaceman shook his head and then knocked on the apartment door.

It was opened almost immediately. The man standing there looked at Spaceman in obvious bewilderment. "Yes?"

"You Devlin Conway?"

"I am. What's going on?"

"I'm Detective Kowalski. L.A.P.D. This is my partner, Detective Maguire."

"We met last night," Blue said.

"Oh, yes, I remember." He didn't look real thrilled with the memory; that could mean he was up to something or maybe he just wasn't that crazy about Blue.

"Can we come in?" Blue said. "There are a few questions we'd like to ask." He kept his tone casual.

Conway still hesitated. "What kind of questions? About what?"

Spaceman got impatient. "Conway, do you really want us to talk to you out here in front of the neighbors?"

He shook his head and stepped aside so that they could come in. As he followed them into the living room, Conway took a deep breath, looking like a man trying to tow himself in, getting control over his emotions. He swept a blanket from the couch and began to fold it. "Okay, Detective Maguire, what can I do for you?"

"The photograph I saw last night. The soldier?"

Conway finished with the blanket and set it aside. His perplexedness at the question might have been genuine. Or it might have a good act. "Excuse me for seeming dense, but those were war pictures, after all. There were a lot of soldiers."

"This one was special to me. I asked you if you knew who he was."

Light dawned in the dark blue eyes. "That one. Well, as I told you then, I have no idea who the boy was. Just a soldier. There were so many."

"That's what you said at the time, yes. But I thought that maybe you answered too quickly. Perhaps if you gave it more thought?"

But Conway shrugged. "Frankly, Detective, I think that the whole question is absurd. What reasonable person would expect me to know such a thing?"

Spaceman saw the overflowing ashtray and so he felt safe in lighting a cigarette of his own. "Okay. Put that aside for the moment. Does the name Wolf mean anything to you?"

Conway didn't move or even change expression at all, but Spaceman saw immediately why Blue had doubted his words. It was in the eyes; less cynical than the rest of his face, they were definitely hiding something. "Wolf? No. Is that his name?"

"We think so. A nickname, probably."

There was an old denim jacket tossed across the back of the couch. Conway picked it up, started to fold it, then tossed it down again. "Well, I'd like to help, of course, but I don't know either the boy in the picture or anyone named Wolf."

Spaceman nodded. He looked around the room, a little surprised to see that beyond one standard furnished apartment painting, the walls were bare. Apparently Conway didn't hang his own pictures. "This is a triple homicide we're working on here," he said almost indifferently. "That may be why we seem to be pressing you so hard."

"A what?" Conway said.

"This Wolf, who we think is the guy in the picture, is a suspect in three recent killings."

"Who?" It came out a little shaky and Conway tried again. "Who is he supposed to have killed?"

"A small-time hood named Vacarro. A Vietnamese refugee named Hua. And Marybeth Wexler, the woman he was shacking up with."

Conway seemed a little paler now. His fingers twisted in the denim jacket again. But he didn't say anything.

Spaceman sensed the sudden vulnerability and moved in to capitalize on it. "You see now why we're so anxious to nab this bastard? To get him before he gets somebody else."

He realized his strategic mistake as soon as the words were out of his mouth and from the look on Blue's face, he knew his partner did, too.

Conway's mouth tightened. "I don't know who the soldier in the photograph is," he said in a hard, flat voice. "I don't know anyone named Wolf. So?"

They would get no more out of him.

Spaceman went through the motions anyway, asking a few more inconsequential questions and receiving monosyllables in reply. Conway was on the defensive now. The news of the murders had shaken him, but there was something even more powerful controlling him.

It was a waste of time.

Outside, Spaceman swung his foot at the curb and connected. "Damn," he said, out of both pain and frustration.

"You really are going to break a toe one of these days." Blue said mildly.

"Yeah, I know," Spaceman replied, limping toward the car. "But I blew that like a goddamned rookie."

"Yes, you did," Blue agreed with maybe too much alacrity. "But it's done now, so we might as well push on."

"Sure, sure. Like that guy pushing the rock up the mountain with his nose or something."

"You mean Sisyphus?"

"What? Yeah, whoever. That's us."

Blue got behind the wheel. "I think maybe we better get down to business with the damned Pentagon. Otherwise, they'll keep jerking us around."

Spaceman groaned. "Jesus, I hate dealing with those assholes."

Blue only nodded with a minimum of sympathy and headed for the office.

38

They met in a small Italian café several blocks from the gallery. Devlin finished his morning-after talk with Addison early and reached the meeting place before Lars. He was halfway through a second glass of wine by the time the fair-haired man arrived.

Lars sat down across from him and grinned. "Okay. Here I am, just as ordered, sir. Why did you leave the message on Tobias' machine that I shouldn't come home?"

Devlin was taken back a little by the word: *home*. Then he leaned forward and spoke softly. "The cops were there. Asking about the picture again."

Lars poured some of the wine into his glass. "That god-damned picture. Why the hell did you hang it anyway?"

Devlin didn't like the tone of his words. He paused before saying anything, so his anger wouldn't show. "Because it's bloody good. I like it. And maybe because it's you and you're my goddamned friend." He hadn't done a very good job of masking his feelings.

Lars pulled back a little. "Hey," he said, startled. "Don't get mad. I'm sorry. It's your fucking picture. That doesn't matter."

Devlin took a deep breath. "They also asked about Wolf," he said after a moment.

Lars massaged the side of his nose thoughtfully; the effects of the beating were almost gone now. "Well, they might have gained a few steps on us, but time is running out." His smile returned faintly. "You were smart to keep me away, just in case they're watching the place. We'll have to make some other plans."

"What does that mean?"

"I don't know yet. I'm working on it. But let's eat first, okay?" He opened the menu and surveyed the price list. "You buying?"

Devlin couldn't help smiling a little now, too. "Yes, of course."

The restaurant was quiet, but he didn't want to talk there about the things that had to be talked about. After lunch was soon enough.

Lars was curious about his suggestion that they drive out to the beach after the meal, but he agreed. Probably he didn't want to risk an argument.

When they were parked in a secluded place overlooking the ocean, Devlin lit a couple of cigarettes, handing one to Lars. They each took a drag.

"Okay, Dev, what's up?"

Devlin leaned both arms against the steering wheel and looked out to where a solitary swimmer was trying to catch a few waves. "The cops told me that Wolf was wanted for three murders. Vacarro I know about. But what about Hua? And some broad. Did you kill them, too?"

Lars was sitting slouched in the seat, staring at the dashboard. His fingers tapped out a restless melody on one knee. "Dev," he said after a long moment, "do you trust me?"

The swimmer disappeared from view. "Yes, of course."

"Then believe me when I say that I haven't done anything that wasn't absolutely necessary."

Devlin wanted to let it go. But he couldn't, not yet. He waited until the swimmer could be seen again, dog-paddling toward shore. "But the woman, Lars? What about that?" Now he turned and looked directly at Lars.

He rubbed his forehead as if it hurt. "Dev, please. Don't press me on this. Sometimes I kill. You've always known that about me, right? I never lied to you about what I am. You watched me kill a lot over there."

"But that was war. It was different."

Lars shook his head, as if he were amused. "Lover, life is a fucking war. Don't you know that yet? Face it."

They were both quiet for a long time. Long enough for the swimmer to leave the water, dry himself, don a pair of jeans and disappear.

"Dev, you understand, don't you?" Lars said finally.

"I'm trying to."

"Shit, if you bail out on me now—"

Devlin shook his head sharply. "There's no question of that, you ass. That's not what I'm saying at all."

"Shit, you had me scared for a minute." Lars grinned, but it was a slightly nervous, unsure kind of smile.

Devlin started the car. "I'm not bailing out," he said.

"Okay. Okay." Lars straightened in the seat. "Find us a phone. I better call Tobias. The three of us need to drop way out of sight until this is over."

Devlin deliberately set aside his doubts; there wasn't any choice, really. "Whatever you say," he muttered. "You're the boss."

It was very late that night before anything at all came back from Washington. Blue, who was hanging around the communications room, ripped off the teletype sheet and took it back to the squad room.

He woke Spaceman with a kick. "Bingo," he said, dropping the sheet on the desk in front of him.

Spaceman scooted upright, belched, rubbed his face with one hand. "Christ, man, have a little pity. My eyes aren't working any more. What the fuck does it say?"

"Well, would you like a name, just for starters?"

"Wolf?"

"Wolf, yes. He is actually one Lars Morgan, former lieutenant in the Special Forces. He was in Nam at the same time Devlin Conway worked for the UPI there."

"Nice."

Blue was looking inordinately pleased with himself. "It gets nicer. I threw another name in, just for the hell of it. And I'll be damned if it didn't turn up. You want to know who else was there, same time, same place?"

"General Westmoreland?" Spaceman hazarded with a somewhat glazed expression.

"Nope. Toby Reardon," Blue said smugly.

Spaceman looked up, startled. "No shit."

"No shit. The memo promises more to follow."

"Well, I'll be damned. Things are getting very interesting. Too bad we still don't know what the hell is going on."

That took a little of the wind out of Maguire's sails. "Yeah, well," he said.

Spaceman stood and stretched. "Tomorrow promises to be a busy day," he said pointedly.

Blue opened his mouth to protest, then closed it again. "How about some dinner?" he said instead. "I could do a couple steaks."

"No business talk?"

He nodded.

Spaceman looked skeptical, but hungry, so he nodded.

39

They had been in the motel room for two days now.

Devlin spent most of his time fiddling with a camera, taking pictures of the room, the other two men, or sometimes it seemed, of nothing at all. Maybe he just liked the way life looked through the lens.

Lars watched television. At least, he kept the set on and he stared at the images. His mind seemed to be elsewhere most of the time.

As for Toby, he was just quietly going crazy. He either paced the room or took an occasional walk across the parking lot and back. A couple times a day they crossed the street to the coffee shop.

Toby thought hell must be something like this.

"Shit," he said finally. "This is really stupid, you know?"

"Hmm?" Lars said, not looking at him.

"I said that hanging around this place is stupid. Dumb. Boring."

"Loosen up, buddy, it's almost over."

"No, it isn't," Toby said glumly. "It will never be over. We're condemned for eternity to this room."

Devlin lifted the camera and pointed it at Toby, snapping still another shot. "If we ever do get out of here," he said, "I'll have enough material for a whole new show. What should I call it?"

"How about 'Three Lunatics in a Cheap Motel'?" Toby muttered.

Lars just laughed softly. "Boy, you would never make it in my line of work anymore. Not with nerves like yours."

Toby turned from the window, where he'd been watching a family of six cram unhappily back into their car. Vacation with the kids and the mother-in-law. Maybe being stuck in here with these two wasn't the worse thing that could happen. "That's an interesting point, Lars. Just what is your so-called line of work anyway?"

Lars glanced at him. "Me? You know damned well what I do. I'm a soldier."

"Right. We've heard all about your years spent tramping through the deadly jungles of the world."

"So?" Lars shifted a little in the chair.

Devlin, seeming to ignore the conversation, dropped onto one knee for a different angle of Lars.

"So I just get the feeling that maybe some of your so-called soldiering might have been done a little closer to home."

"Such as?" Lars seemed almost amused by the talk; maybe he was just glad to have the boredom broken.

"Meaning that you seem to know your way around this world we're in pretty good."

Lars leaned forward and punched the television off. He got up and walked over to where Toby was standing. "Hey, lover boy, you know everybody makes his way the best he knows how to. Dev has his camera. You make your living with your cock and I use a goddamned gun. Maybe my way is not as good as Dev's. Or even yours. But what the hell difference does it make at this particular point in time?"

Toby shrugged. "None, I guess."

Lars grinned and gave him a one-armed hug. "Right, Tobias."

Devlin got the shot.

☐   ☐   ☐

"We could get into trouble for this," Blue whispered for the fifth time in the last twenty minutes.

"Yes, Mother, I know that," Spaceman muttered through gritted teeth. "But do you have any better ideas?"

"No."

"So stand the fuck still will you, please?"

Spaceman was crouched down, shielded by Blue's body as he worked on the lock. Finally something snapped and the door opened. They stepped into the cabin of Toby Reardon's boat.

There wasn't much to see, beyond the artifacts of a middle-class consumer's life. Bed, table, a couple of chairs. Television, stereo, video recorder. A shelf that held books, records, tapes. A closet crammed with clothes.

Blue looked around and sighed. "Big deal. It was sure worth all the effort getting in here, right?"

Spaceman just grunted. He sat by the phone and hit the button of the answering machine. First they heard Reardon's voice. "Sorry, but I'm out of town until further notice. All appointments have been canceled." Spaceman snorted. "Think about all those disappointed broads." He hit another button to see if there were any incoming messages. A couple of women had called, but nobody left a name. Then he straightened as Conway's voice emerged. "Toby, if Lars is still with you—tell him not to come back here. Meet me at Luigi's for lunch." That was all.

Blue was leaning against the counter. "So they met and then they vanished, all three of them."

"Yeah." Spaceman glanced at him. "So much for your artist friend."

"I guess." Blue shook his head. "Are we done here?"

"Apparently." Spaceman rifled through some papers on the table next to the phone, but found nothing that seemed to bear on the case. "You know," he said almost absently, "if something doesn't happen pretty soon on this thing, McGannon is going to shove it away."

Blue, halfway out the door, stopped. "You mean that?"

"I'm surprised he hasn't been giving us flack already."

"We have three murders here."

"But none of them are very important." He locked the door again and followed Blue onto the dock. "Best thing we can do," he said, only half joking, "is hope for somebody else to get wasted."

Blue got into the car and slammed the door with undue force.

It was after eleven that night when they finally left the motel and climbed into Devlin's Pontiac. Lars drove, with Devlin sitting next to him and Toby in the back seat. Each man was now armed. Lars had produced the weapons earlier, not revealing where they had come from. Nobody asked.

They didn't say much to one another during the ride out to McCallister Field, a small private airport northeast of the city. There was only one wooden building at the far end of the single runway; it was lit, but otherwise the field was in darkness.

A battered black van was parked next to the building. Inside there seemed to be only one shadowy figure moving around.

Lars stopped the car at the opposite end of the field and turned off the engine. "You two stay here," he ordered in a low voice, although whoever was inside the shack could not possibly have heard. "When the runway lights come on, deploy just like I told you. Okay?"

"Where are you going?" Devlin asked.

"Recon." He checked the Walther beneath his jacket, then took the Uzi machine gun, tucked it under one arm, and got out of the car. In only an instant, he had vanished into the darkness.

Toby leaned over the seat and spoke, his lips practically touching Devlin's ear. "He's so damned good at this that it's scary. Really scary."

Devlin just nodded.

It was a couple more minutes before they heard what sounded like a single shot ring out. Neither man said anything; they didn't even look at one another. Strangely, neither even thought of the possibility that it had been Lars who'd gotten shot.

At exactly five minutes after one, the lights along the runway suddenly blazed on. Devlin waited the space of one deep breath, then said, "Let's move."

Toby nodded.

They got out of the car and walked along the runway to the place Lars had indicated earlier. With a nod, they parted, going to opposite sides of the runway and then stretching out in the damp grass. They drew the guns.

Devlin's mouth was dry. He tried to work up a little spit, just so he could swallow, but it wasn't easy. A second later, he could hear the sound of a small plane circling overhead. Once, twice it went around the field. The lights on the plane blinked three times and the field lights answered by going off once and coming back on.

The Cessna finally came in and made a rather bumpy landing. It rolled to a stop just short of where Devlin and Toby were waiting. Devlin wiped a trickle of sweat from his face. The plane's door opened and three men got out. Two were dressed in cheap black suits that seemed strained to the breaking point over their matching Sherman-tank bodies. The third was a much smaller man, dapper, and obviously the one in charge. There was a black briefcase chained to his wrist. All three men started toward the van, talking audibly in rapid French.

Devlin raised the gun a little, hoping to hell he wouldn't have to use it.

When the window in the shack suddenly shattered, everybody outside jumped, including Devlin. Before the two gorillas could react further, a short burst of Uzi fire from inside the shack cut them both down. The little man with the briefcase turned and started to run.

Devlin took one more breath, then jumped up, gun held at shoulder level. "Stop!" he yelled, noticing with one part of his mind that Toby was up on the other side of the runway.

The man stopped.

"Don't move," Devlin urged him. "Lars?" he yelled over one shoulder.

The door opened and Lars emerged, the Uzi swinging from one hand as he walked toward them, in no hurry. The Frenchman stood very still, only his eyes betraying any sign of life.

Devlin could hear the raspy sound of Toby breathing across the way.

Lars reached them finally. "Well, well," he said with mock cheer. "If it isn't my old friend Jacques. Long time no see. Beirut, wasn't it?"

Jacques looked at him bitterly. "Fool," he said, then he spit.

Lars only laughed.

"Why did you not kill me with those two?"

"Because I wanted to be sure you had the stones first. You want to take the case off, please?"

"I have the diamonds." He made no move toward the case, however.

"I can always just cut it off. Of course, that might also mean cutting off the arm."

Jacques sneered. "You and your silly games, Wolf. I know very well that you are going to kill me. So do it now and take the diamonds. For all the good they will do you."

"I expect them to do me a lot of good," Lars said easily. He reached inside his jacket, pulled out the Walther and put it to the back of Jacques's head. He pulled the trigger.

"Jesus," Toby said. Then he turned away and threw up.

Devlin just stood there.

Lars knelt to search through the dead man's pockets, finally pulling out a ring with two small keys. One key freed the case from the chain. "Halfway home," Lars mumbled to himself. In another instant, he had the case open. Inside there was only one thing, a black velvet bag.

"Shit," he said.

He opened the drawstring of the bag and carefully dumped the contents onto the smooth surface of the runway.

Devlin caught his breath at the way the diamonds captured and held the bright lights. Toby had quit heaving and now he moved forward for a better look. "My God," he whispered. "They're beautiful."

Lars ran a finger through the stones. "JesusohJesus," he said, sounding almost tearful. Then he looked up. "Didn't I tell you guys? Didn't I promise?"

"You promised," Devlin said flatly.

Toby just shook his head. He picked up one of the diamonds and walked a few steps away.

Devlin crouched next to Lars, but didn't touch the stones or look at the dead man.

Lars patted him on the thigh. "You okay?"

"Yes. I'm okay."

Lars smiled. "We did it, lover."

Devlin only nodded.

40

Blue carefully poured more wine into the glass that was balanced on the edge of the hot tub. This made one drink too many. He didn't really give a damn. It had been a very long day and not a good one. True to Spaceman's prediction, McGannon was making noises about forgetting the case, moving on to something new. There was no lack of fresh murders to occupy their time.

Water splashed as Blue kicked angrily. This was his case, damnit, and McGannon couldn't just pull the plug on the investigation. Of course, McGannon could do just that if he wanted to and the realization that there wasn't one damned thing Blue Maguire could do about it was the reason he was sulking in the hot tub and swallowing too much L'Enfant Jesus 1929.

He heard the doorbell and thought about ignoring it. But, finally, with a sigh, he leaned out of the tub and pressed the intercom button. "What?"

"Blue?"

"Come on in," he said wearily.

Spaceman used his own key to open the door. A moment later, he appeared on the balcony. "Little cool for swimming, isn't it?"

"Not in here."

Spaceman just nodded.

"Was there something you wanted?"

"Not especially. I was just feeling bugged about this damned case."

Blue grimaced. "Join the club." He sipped some of the wine. "You want to hear the funny part? I can't even remember what the Wexler broad looked like anymore. So much for my frigging cause célèbre."

"Your what?"

He shook his head. "Never mind. Have a drink, why don't you?"

Spaceman went for a glass, then came back and poured some wine, which he gulped down in two swallows. "Not bad," he said.

"Thank you."

Spaceman poured some more. "Those three guys have to be somewhere."

"True. But they're not on Reardon's boat. Or in Conway's apartment. Addison doesn't know anything." The gallery owner was in quite a state, because his newest star was apparently lost somewhere in the galaxy. Blue splashed water again. "Shit."

Perversely, the madder he got, the cooler Spaceman seemed to become. "Oh, well," he said now, "they'll turn up."

The phone rang.

"Maybe that's them now."

Blue made no move to answer the call. He didn't want to, not tonight, his mood was low enough already.

"Want me to get it?" Spaceman said after two more rings.

"I don't care," Blue muttered. "Go head, answer the damned thing."

Spaceman lifted the receiver. "Maguire's," he said. He gave a small shrug. "Hung up."

"Good."

"That guy still calling?"

"Once in a while." Blue shrugged. "Like every night. I've got a short list of possibles on it. Social Security is checking them for me." He drained the glass and sat up. "Forget it. You want something to eat?"

"Whatcha got?"

"Lasagna."

"Okay, sure."

A few minutes later they were in the kitchen and the lasagna was disappearing rapidly. "You know," Spaceman said through a bite, "I'm thinking about having Lainie move in with me. What do you think?"

"Sounds good. If you want it."

"Yeah, I do," Spaceman said, but there was some doubt in the words. "I mean, one minute I do and the next I start to wonder."

Blue shoved his plate aside. "Well, I'll tell you, partner, I'm not exactly the one to come to for advice in the romance department."

Spaceman looked at him, but before he could say anything, the phone rang again. Spaceman raised a brow. Blue just shrugged helplessly and answered it.

Spaceman kept eating while Blue listened and jotted down something on a memo pad by the phone. He hung up after a moment. "Well, I don't think we have to worry about McGannon shutting down the case," he said grimly.

"Oh?"

"This looks like it belongs to us."

Spaceman smiled. "Told you they'd be back." He didn't even bother to ask what had happened. Instead, he just concentrated on finishing the meal while Blue went to don shoes and socks.

The bodies, four of them, had all been piled inside a small building at the airport. Two of the dead had been machine-gunned, but the others were dead of single gunshots to the back of their heads, with what might have been a Walther. It might not have been, too, but Blue would have bet the rent money. One of the dead was a Vietnamese and the others, according to their papers, were French.

Spaceman toyed with a length of chain that was attached to one of the men. "Looks like Wolf got whatever they were carrying."

"Drugs?" Blue ventured tentatively.

"I doubt it. This shrimp couldn't carry enough on his wrist to make all this trouble worthwhile. I'd say something smaller but very valuable."

Blue surveyed the grisly scene. "I wonder if Conway and Reardon really know what the hell is going on."

"Of course they do," Spaceman said scornfully. "And I'm going to bring all three of the fuckers down. We're going to do it," he amended.

"Yeah, right," Blue said. "We're going to bring the fuckers down. Soon as we can find them."

41

Lars was almost morbidly fascinated by the diamonds. He could sit for hours at the table, toying with the bits of shiny stone, watching the play of light caused by the sun. Devlin gave in to his request for some pictures of their treasure.

Toby, meanwhile, kept the television on, waiting for some news about the killings at the airport. He was beginning to think that the damned bodies were never going to be found, when finally a report showed up on the morning news. He was the only one in the room who listened. When the news was replaced by "I Love Lucy," he killed the volume. "What next?" he asked.

The blunt question hung in the air.

Lars quit fooling with the diamonds and smiled. "Practical Tobias. That's why I love you, man, because there's just no bullshit. You always get right to the point. What next. Good question."

"And I imagine that you have a good answer for me?"

"How about: I'm working on it. While you were out for breakfast before I set up a meet with Tran. In about"—he glanced at his watch—"ninety minutes, in fact. He wants his cut and I want him to do something for us."

"Which is?"

"To find out if his people would be interested in buying the stones back from us."

Toby stared at him in apparent awe. "Christ, Lars, first you rip them off and now you want to deal? You have got more balls than anybody I ever met."

"Thanks." Then Lars frowned. "Didn't you say something once about how it doesn't take brains to have balls?"

"I might have said something like that." Toby smirked and turned back to watch Lucy stomp grapes.

"Funny man," Lars muttered. He headed for the can to shower and shave, then paused in the doorway. "One of you comes with me. The other stays with the goodies."

Toby and Lars arrived nearly fifteen minutes early for the meet with Tran. Lars said that was just the way he liked it. Toby parked behind the deserted fish market. "This place stinks," he bitched. "Couldn't we meet this joker someplace clean?"

Lars nodded absently, his attention obviously elsewhere. Something in his posture or expression alerted Toby. "What's wrong?"

He shrugged. "Don't know. Probably nothing." After another moment of silent watchfulness, he went on wryly, "Occupational hazard. Paranoia." He pulled out the Walther and hefted it thoughtfully. "My security blanket. You wait here, Tobias. Anything happens that doesn't seem quite kosher, do what you can."

"Which means?"

"Which means save my ass, baby." With that, Lars slid out of the car and walked toward the building.

Toby watched him go, chewing on his lower lip. Great. Just fucking great. Save his ass. He didn't even have the damned gun. Should have brought it, of course. Lars probably thought he had. But just holding the thing made him nervous and this was just supposed to be a meet with Phillipe Tran. How could that turn into trouble?

But now he was in charge of covering Lars Morgan's crazy ass. And just suppose something happened and Lars got blown away. That would leave him and Devlin Conway on the run with a shitload of very hot rocks. Not even to mention that if he had to go back to the frigging motel and report that Morgan was permanently removed, Conway would probably get very upset.

The end of the gun barrel planted itself firmly just behind Toby's ear and all thought stopped briefly. When there was no immediate explosion, however, no sudden end, he started to think again.

Damn, was what he thought. It was getting a little tiresome the way people kept poking deadly weapons into various parts of his anatomy. I'm a lover, not a fighter, he wanted to tell the world at large.

"You will please step from the car," a very soft voice said. "Carefully, because I would not like to pull the trigger quite yet."

"Sure thing, buddy," Toby said. He opened the door and got out slowly. With the damned gun again jammed into his ear, they started awkwardly toward the building.

Lars was apparently inside.

By the time they were about halfway to the door, Toby was mad. He didn't like to lose his temper, but enough, damnit, was definitely enough.

Lars Morgan, after all, wasn't the only one who'd been in the frigging Special Forces and who knew a few tricks. Toby smiled to himself.

An instant later, he pulled the famous fake-stumble routine. There was always the chance that the damned gun would go off in a reflex move, but this time it didn't. The gook ended up on the ground, out cold, without ever knowing what had hit him.

Toby flexed the fingers of his right hand thoughtfully, pleased with himself. All those broads who paid for his stud services never knew what they had, the stupid cunts. Well, he was done with that kind of shit now.

He took the gun from the fallen man and continued toward the building. The door was cracked open and he peered inside, the smell of old fish hitting him strongly. He could see Lars, pacing the concrete floor and smoking, apparently waiting. Toby almost called out to him, but at the last moment, he caught the flash of movement in the loft overhead.

Toby pushed the door open a little more and slipped inside. As he watched, the figure above knelt and took aim at Lars. Scarcely even thinking about what he was doing, Toby jerked the appropriated gun into position and fired.

He saw Phillipe Tran pitch forward and fall through the air. But at the same time, he was aware of Lars whipping around toward him, the Walther raised.

"Don't shoot!" Toby screamed. "It's me!"

After an endless moment, Lars lowered his gun.

Toby wiped his mouth with the back of one hand.

They both walked over to stare down at Tran.

"He dead?" Toby said hoarsely.

"Very. Good shot. You haven't lost your touch."

Toby fought down the wave of nausea that threatened. "Christ, I didn't want to kill anybody."

Lars glanced at him. "The bastard was trying to shaft us, Tobias. To do us in. You've got nothing to feel bad about."

Toby just shook his head.

"Where'd that gun come from?"

"Guy outside."

"You off him?"

Toby wiped his mouth again. "No. No, I did not off him. Cold-cocked, is all." He held the gun out and Lars took it.

"Well, let's get the hell out of here before the rest of the goddamned Vietnamese army shows up."

They walked outside and over to where the unconscious man was. Lars wiped all possible prints from the gun and then pressed it once more into the owner's hand. "This creep killed the guy inside. You got that, Tobias?"

"What?" he said dumbly.

Lars gave his shoulder a painful squeeze. "No matter what

happens, you never say one word about who did it. Never. They can't touch you. Okay?''

"Okay."

Toby knew what was going to happen when Lars took out his own gun and pressed it to the back of the man's head. The crack of the shot barely even made him jump. It was scary to realize how familiar this was all becoming. Very scary, and by the time they were back to the car, Toby was shivering uncontrollably.

Lars got behind the wheel.

Toby felt like an ass, but he couldn't stop shaking. "Damn," he said through chattering teeth. "What the fuck is wrong with me?"

Lars didn't start the car. Instead, he turned and looked at Toby. "Take a couple deep breaths," he said. "Slow, careful, steady." His voice was quiet and kind, an absurdity coming from a man who seconds before had committed still another cold-blooded murder.

Toby tried to take the advice. The first few breaths he took were raspy and shaky, but then he seemed to get control again. The air came more easily.

"Better?" Lars said.

"Yeah, I think."

"Okay. It's been a long time for you, I know." He turned the key in the ignition. "By the way, thanks."

Toby just looked at him.

"For saving my ass."

He leaned against the car door and closed his eyes. "Just repaying an old debt," he said. "From that day in DaNang."

42

Blue received the information back from Social Security in record time, with no explanation for the unprecedented promptness. Maybe it was because he hadn't gone through the regular channels; he'd just gotten in touch with a guy who used to work for the old man and who was now a government appointee. Sometimes it paid to be somebody.

On his way back to the squad room, where he was definitely not somebody, Blue checked over the list of four names. He zeroed in on one immediately: Danny Morell, of Detroit. Motor City, had to be it. He tried to remember Morell and finally managed the vague image of a stocky, dark man with a ready grin.

He reached the desk.

Much as he wanted to pursue this, it was time to work now. It was more important to find Wolf and his friends than to track down an old war buddy. Blue folded the paper and put it into his shirt pocket. He held up the new teletype sheets. "Some more dope from our friends in the Pentagon," he said.

Spaceman grunted, busy removing the cellophane from a sticky jelly doughnut.

Blue sat, looking at him. "Thought you were going to lose fifteen pounds."

"Ten. Ten pounds. Besides, it's not New Year's until tomorrow at midnight."

"Hmmph." Blue was reading the memo from Washington. "Lars Morgan was kicked out of the Special Forces for 'exceeding standard operating procedures.' I guess that means he was too violent even for them. Can you imagine?"

Spaceman licked a finger thoughtfully. "All it really means is that he was too good at his job. He did what they wanted done, what the motherfuckers taught him to do, and when things got messy, they bailed out on him."

Blue frowned. "For some reason, you keep sounding sympathetic to this bastard."

"No, not sympathetic. Just honest. Can you deny the truth of what I'm saying?"

"I guess not." He looked at the paper again. "Sergeant Tobias Reardon testified for Morgan at the hearing, but it didn't help. Since then, Morgan's been reported to be working as a mercenary in various trouble spots around the world."

Spaceman finished the doughnut. He snickered. "So he took the recruiting ads seriously. He joined the service and learned a skill."

"Seems like."

"No wonder the bastard is running circles around a couple of dumb cops like us." The phone rang. Spaceman grinned. "Right on time."

"You're a son of a bitch, Kowalski."

"Yeah." He picked up the receiver. "Kowalski. What?" He listened for a moment, then grunted in response, and hung up. "Guess what?"

Blue threw the teletype down wearily. "Don't tell me."

"Okay," Spaceman said agreeably. "I'll let you see for yourself."

He didn't like what he saw at the abandoned fish market. This guy Morgan or Wolf, whoever the hell, was playing havoc with the damned crime statistics for the year. It was possible he had killed just one of the two dead men, but Blue wasn't ready to believe that.

They didn't stay around the murder scene very long. The next stop was even less pleasant: They had to go across town to the Viet refugee center to tell Angel Tran that her brother Phillipe was dead. Maybe this time she would show a little more interest in the case, Blue thought bitterly.

Then he felt bad about the thought.

But still. . . .

Miss Tran was obviously annoyed when she looked up from the typewriter and saw the same two cops standing in front of her desk. "What is it this time?" she said with forced politeness.

Blue told her, bluntly.

Her beautiful and closed face just closed a little more. She didn't say anything.

Spaceman leaned one hip on the edge of the desk. "Do you have any idea what your brother was into, Miss Tran, that might have led to this?"

She shrugged. "Phillipe sold vegetables."

"Nobody put a bullet in your brother because the eggplant wasn't fresh," Spaceman said sharply. "There must be something else."

Miss Tran was playing with a bottle of White-Out correction fluid. "Phillipe was into the California version of the American dream, Detective Kowalski. He wanted to get into the fast lane and make it big."

"How was he planning to do that?" Spaceman asked.

"I do not know." Her voice was flat.

He glanced at Blue, who shrugged, and said, "We'll probably be in touch. You'll have to go down and identify the body."

"I can do that."

They started for the door.

"I'm the last one left," she said suddenly.

Blue stopped. "I'm sorry?"

"My father died in Saigon and my mother on the boat

coming over. Now that Phillipe is gone, I'm the last one left of my family.''

"That's too bad," he said. "You ought to think about helping us find whoever killed your brother, maybe."

She only looked at him.

Spaceman was waiting on the porch. "Nobody will tell us anything," he said. "Have you noticed that?"

"I've noticed. It's as if there's a big secret that everybody knows but you and me."

Spaceman seemed to resist visibly the urge to kick the step as they headed toward the car.

43

Lars had been chewing on the pencil for almost an hour. There were little flecks of yellow paint around his mouth. So far, he hadn't written a word on the motel stationery on the desk in front of him.

No one had said anything in all that time. Toby was stretched out on one of the beds, hands behind his head, staring at the ceiling. Devlin was in a chair, feet propped on the desk, watching Lars destroy the Ticonderoga number two.

"Tran and his bunch tried to screw us," Lars finally said around the pencil. He made it sound like a big announcement.

"Agreed," Toby said to the ceiling. "Actually, though, Lars, I could have told you that a long time ago."

Devlin didn't say anything.

"I don't want us to have anything else to do with those Saigon scumbags."

"Smart decision," Toby said dryly. He seemed perversely determined to aggravate Lars. An old game with him.

Lars took the battered pencil out of his mouth and pointed it at him. "Are you interested in taking charge, sweetheart?" he said.

Toby raised a hand in mock surrender.

"I think," Lars continued after a moment, "that we'll try

the other side of the street. Before we start trying to fence the damned things ourselves.''

Devlin cleared his throat. "When you say the other side of the street, what you mean is Delvecchio, right? You're going to try and sell the diamonds directly to him.''

Lars smiled, a teacher proud of a bright student, and tossed the pencil into the air, catching it again. "Bingo.''

Toby sat up, pulling both knees to his chest and resting his chin on them. "Are you under the impression that Delvecchio is a fan of yours? Or that you can trust him any more than you could Tran's group?''

"No, Tobias, I'm not that fucking naive. But there is one crucial difference.''

"Which you will now tell us.''

"Tran and his friends were amateurs. Lousy amateurs. They didn't know shit about the real world. Tran never understood the subtleties of a deal like this.''

Toby snickered. "And you think that Delvecchio, the fucking godfather for Chrissake, is a subtle man?''

"I think that he understands a business deal.''

Unexpectedly, Toby shrugged his agreement. "Okay. We don't have anything to lose. It can hardly get worse.''

Lars didn't comment on that. He just looked at Devlin; apparently this was a democracy where everybody got an equal vote.

"Whatever,'' Devlin said. He shook his head, smiling faintly. "I'm way out of my depth here. You two are the soldiers. I just take pictures, remember?''

"How do we reach Delvecchio?'' Toby said.

"We don't,'' Lars replied. "Nobody reaches Papa D. What we do is put ourselves in a position to be reached by him. I have a feeling it won't be hard to do.''

"Sort of like pretending to be a duck in a shooting gallery, right?''

Lars only smiled. "Time to draw straws again, lads. Somebody has to stay here with the goodies and the other lucky bastard gets to come play duckie with me.''

Devlin brought his feet to the floor. "I'll go this time. Toby can babysit the glass."

Lars nodded, showing neither pleasure nor otherwise with the choice, then he picked up the Styrofoam bucket and headed for the ice machine.

Toby uncurled from his place on the bed. "You get off on providing target practice for the dagos, buddy?"

Devlin shrugged. "Things are crazy, Toby."

"True."

"I think we're either going to get very rich here or else the whole thing is going to fall apart in a big hurry. If that happens, I think I'd much rather be right in the front line."

Toby nodded, understanding.

"You're telling me that the Mafia really comes here?" Devlin said. "I mean, it looks like something out of a gangster movie."

Lars was eating a plate of ravioli. "Bad movies are sometimes more like real life than good ones." he said.

The restaurant had a lot of brass and wood and private booths. Most of the customers were men in dark suits. Devlin, who couldn't seem to find an appetite, was drinking a glass of the house red.

Lars put down the fork and took a sip of beer. "You scared?" he asked suddenly.

Devlin looked up, startled. "No. Yes." He shrugged. "I guess so."

"Good. Only an idiot wouldn't be scared, and I never thought you were stupid."

"You seem cool enough."

"Ha, don't let this Mike Hammer exterior fool you. I'm not all that brave, either."

Before Devlin could say anymore, they were joined by another man, a skinny, ferretlike individual in khaki pants and a Hawaiian shirt. "We got some special offerings in the private dining room, if you gentlemen would come with me.''

They looked at one another, then stood simultaneously. The ferret took them through the hot and noisy kitchen, into a much smaller room. This one was empty, except for a single wooden table and two chairs. One of the chairs was occupied by Delvecchio. On either side of him were two of the Cro-Magnon types who had come to Toby's boat on Christmas.

Lars sat in the empty chair without waiting for an invitation to do so. He relaxed, legs crossed, and lit a cigarette. Devlin stood next to him. As always, when he didn't have a camera to hold, his arms seemed to be useless, awkward appendages.

Delvecchio was eating a bowl of oatmeal. ''My gut,'' he said in apparent explanation. ''Shot to hell.''

''Too bad,'' Lars said indifferently.

The old man took another bite of the cereal and very carefully licked the spoon clean. Then he set it down. ''I am tired of having to deal with you, Wolf. There will be no dialogue. You have certain items that rightfully belong to me. I want them back.''

Lars smiled brightly. ''Terrific. All you need to do is pay me four million dollars and we never have to see each other again. Believe me, I'm just as tired of you as you are of me.''

Devlin watched, as always, in a sort of awe at the way Lars handled himself. The bastard was one hell of a performer.

Delvecchio, however, didn't seem much impressed. ''I seen a lot of tough guys like you over the years,'' he said, folding the linen napkin. ''All chutzpah and no smarts.''

''Takes no brains to have balls,'' Lars said. ''Balls is gentile talk for chutzpah. I may have no smarts, Papa, but I have got your fucking diamonds, right?''

''You really expect me to pay you for something that is already mine by rights?''

''I could always put them on the open market.''

"You could do that," Delvecchio agreed. "Of course doing it might get you killed."

Lars smiled. "Walking across Sunset could get me killed."

Delvecchio was quiet for a moment. "We both seem to be in a touchy situation," he said finally.

Lars nodded. "Look," he said, "I don't want to be an ass about this. Why don't I give you a break? Three million and the stones are yours. Is that a bargain or what?"

The old man thought about it. "I'll be in touch," he said.

"Soon," Lars said. "How about within twenty-four hours? You meet my price by then or the diamonds will go to the highest bidder."

Delvecchio almost smiled. "You're one for the books, Wolf. I begin to think that maybe you're working for somebody else. If I knew for sure, and who that somebody might be, perhaps you might be dead already." He waved a hand impatiently.

That seemed to end the meeting and the geek in the Magnum PI shirt showed them out.

Devlin parked directly in front of their room, sliding in next to Toby's VW. He didn't say anything and neither did Lars, who knocked on the door so that Toby could take the chain off.

A sound came from inside the room, not the chain sliding from the door, not anything that they could identify. But it was not a good sound. "Oh, shit," Lars said quietly. When he tried the knob and it turned easily, he said it again, more softly, more savagely.

Devlin wanted to stop him. He didn't want to see what was on the other side of the door, but Lars gave a push and they stepped in.

The room was a shambles, torn up, every damned thing seemingly destroyed. Lars expelled his breath in a loud sigh. They picked their way through the rubble carefully, moving toward the bathroom.

Toby was in there.

Devlin thought at first that he was dead, like all the others, and he was only surprised at how unsurprised he was. Sudden and violent death seemed to be the natural order of things now.

But finally the bloody form moved a little, groaning, the same sound they had heard from outside the room. Lars moved quickly to the toilet tank, the top of which was in pieces on the floor, and peered in hopelessly. The diamonds were gone, of course. Then he came to help Devlin lift Toby and carry him back into the bedroom, where they lowered him carefully onto one of the ravaged mattresses.

Toby seemed more alert by this time. His head tossed restlessly from side to side. "Fuckers," he said in a thick voice. A thin trail of spittle and blood ran out of his mouth when he talked. " . . . fuckers messed up my face . . . can't make money without my face . . . goddamn them . . ."

Devlin went back into the bathroom, pulled a towel from underneath a pile of stuff, and wet it in the bathtub. He returned to kneel on the mattress and began to wipe Toby's face. "I don't think anything's broken, Toby," he said reassuringly. "You'll be okay."

"My face?"

"It's okay, really. That perfect profile is still there." He ran both hands over Toby's body, noticing when the other man flinched. "You might have a cracked rib, though." He lifted his head and looked at Lars.

He was standing in the middle of the room, staring around as if the destruction of the motel room also meant the end of much more. Then he shrugged and straightened his shoulders. "Clean the bastard up," he said wearily. "I'll go across the street to the drugstore and get what you need."

"He probably needs a doctor."

"Huh-uh. Unless he wants us to just drop him at the emergency room and take off." It was a question directed at Toby himself.

The bloodied form raised itself a little from the mattress.

"Hell, no," he said. He spit blood. "I want those fuckers. They took our diamonds and they did this to me. I want them, damnit."

"Who?" Lars said softly.

Toby wiped at the mucus dripping from his nose. "It was the goddamned Viet mafia."

"Who else?" Devlin said. "You know what we are, Lars? Just a goddamned Ping-Pong ball for Delvecchio and Tran's people to hit back and forth. And in case you don't know it, the bloody ball never wins the game, mate."

Lars just shrugged and started for the door.

"Lars?" Toby said.

He paused. "What?"

"I'm sorry about the stones."

Lars kicked a shattered chair leg out of his path. "Don't you worry, Tobias," he said in an icy voice. "We'll get the diamonds back. And we'll put their frigging balls in the wringer for what they did to you." He looked at Devlin. "Get ready to split. Soon as we have him patched up, we better look for a safe place to stay."

"Is there one?"

Lars smiled, although his eyes were empty of expression. "Sure, lover. You're safe with me."

44

It was early when the phone rang.

Blue woke up reluctantly. It took a moment for him to remember that he'd fallen asleep on the couch waiting for a call. That was after he'd tried to phone Morell, but gotten no answer. His mouth tasted of brandy, good stuff, but despoiled now by several hours of restless sleep and bad dreams. He worked up a little saliva and spit into the snifter before lifting the receiver and making a reasonably appropriate sound into it.

"Blue? You awake?"

"No," he said.

"Well, listen anyway. We've got a lead."

"Oh, it's you."

"Who the hell did you think it was?" Spaceman said irritably. "Fucking J. Edgar Hoover? Do you want to hear this or not?"

"Hoover's dead, you know. And yes, I want to hear it. I'm breathless with anticipation."

"Reardon's car turned up. Outside a motel on Santa Monica. A zone car spotted the license and they're sitting on it for us. You want to pick me up?"

"Okay." Blue hung up.

He was halfway to the bathroom before the realization hit that he was starting to act just like his partner. Blue had always been a man who put great faith in the amenities of civilization. Simple things, like saying hello and good-bye and thank you.

God, he thought, standing frozen in the hallway, I'm turning into Kowalski.

That thought shook him up. So much so, that he took a shower lasting several minutes longer than it should have under the circumstances, shaved with particular attention, and gargled three times with Listerine to kill the taste and smell of old booze. Finally, he dressed with care in grey flannel slacks, crisp white shirt, and his best blue blazer. A new tie.

He felt much better for all the effort, even when he pulled up in front of the apartment building on Vermont and found an impatient Kowalski fuming.

Spaceman jumped into the car and slammed the door eloquently. "You took long enough."

"Sorry," he said, although it wasn't true.

"Where's the frigging party?"

"What party?"

"The one you're obviously done up for." Blue glanced at him, at the seedy sport coat and cords. "It is New Year's Eve in few hours," he said mildly. "I just want to be ready."

Spaceman snorted.

They sent the zone car back onto patrol and then Spaceman crawled around inside Reardon's VW carefully. Nothing much came of the search. Several magazines—*Video Review, Ellery Queen's Mystery Magazine, The New Yorker*. A half-eaten roll of Tropical Fruit Lifesavers. A well-creased map of Beverly Hills.

"Big time hustler," Spaceman muttered in disgust.

Blue was just back from a visit to the manager's office. "You were expecting maybe whips and strawberry body lotion?" He perched on the front of the car. "I talked to the manager, a Mr. Harold Brown. He told me that there were three men staying in the room. They had another car, a Le Mans, but since Reardon actually rented the room, all he had was a record of this license. They left very early this morning, all three of them, in the other car."

"Great."

Blue absently rubbed the RR hood ornament on the VW. "He also passed along the information that several other guests complained about some noise coming from this room last night."

"What was it?"

"Mr. Brown didn't know. To quote him, 'They shut up afore I could get over there, and anyways, I ain't no fucking cop.' So he never checked. He gave me a key."

Which, as it turned out, they didn't need, because the door wasn't locked.

"Christ," Spaceman said from the threshold. "Some noise? I wonder what they would have called World War II?"

Blue made his way through the mess, following a trail of blood that ended in the bathroom. "No body anyway," he said.

"That's a switch." Spaceman nudged some rubble with his foot. "I guess we better get a lab crew over here and let them dig through this mess."

"Better them than me," Blue said. Then he bent and moved aside the remains of a lamp. He came up with an exposed roll of film, still in its cannister. "Conway can't stop taking pictures," he said. For some reason, it was a thought that made him feel a sudden sadness.

They took one more quick look around the room, then stepped out. This time, Spaceman locked the door securely.

"What do you think happened in there?" Blue asked, leaning against the Porsche as Spaceman reached in toward the radio.

"It's my guess that we're not the only ones looking for

Morgan and his two sidekicks. Except that whoever else is looking found them first."

Blue nodded. "Maybe we should hire whoever it is for the department," he said. "You and I seem to be the only ones in town who can't find Morgan."

45

They were still just riding around in the Pontiac. Lars couldn't seem to settle down anyplace. Safety for now was inside this car, on the move. Devlin was next to him, silent and watchful, the smashed camera on the seat between them.

In the back seat, Toby stretched out as best he could, trying to find a spot on his body that didn't hurt. It was a losing battle. Lars had kindly provided, in addition to the iodine and bandages, a bottle of pretty good Scotch to help the pain. Toby, however, kept the sips small and infrequent, because he figured this was not a very good time to be drunk.

Abruptly Lars pulled into the parking lot of a McDonald's and let the engine idle. "I've been thinking," he said.

"About a Big Mac?" Devlin said. "That's great. Our lives are hanging by a very thin thread and you want special sauce."

Toby laughed shortly, then wished that he hadn't.

Lars gave Devlin a dirty look, then shook his head. "No, fool. I've been thinking that there's a piece missing someplace and it just came to me who it is."

"Who?"

"Tran's sister. What the fuck was her name?"

Nobody remembered.

Lars reached over the seat and pulled up a battered briefcase. He fumbled through the contents and came up with the black notebook. "Angel," he said after a moment. "Stupid name. Angel Tran."

"What's her involvement?" Devlin asked.

"I don't know. But there must be something. Now that I think about it, Phillipe wasn't bright enough to be in something like this on his own." He shrugged. "Somebody else had to be telling him what to do, and I like the sister."

"You know where she is, I suppose?" Toby said.

Lars lifted the book. "Of course."

"You have all of us in that damned book?"

He just smiled.

Toby lifted the bottle in tribute. "You're amazing, Lars. You could have gone far in life."

Lars glanced back at him in surprise. "I have gone far, Tobias."

"What's it say about me in that book?"

"None of your damned business."

Since they were there anyway, they pulled up to the drive-through window and got some burgers.

They parked across the street from something called the Los Angeles Vietnamese Center, and looked out at the building, which seemed deserted.

"Maybe she's not here today," Toby said. "It is New Year's Eve."

"She'll be here. For one thing, she lives upstairs. And for another, her brother just died, so it's not likely she'll be out partying, right?"

Toby slumped back against the seat. "I forgot about that," he mumbled, suddenly paler beneath the bruises.

Lars gave him a quick thumbs-up gesture, and after a moment, he smiled fleetingly. Lars opened the car door and got out, then leaned in through the window. "You two wait here."

"You sure?" Devlin said.

"I can handle the broad. You just keep your eyes open."

They watched him cross the street and go into the building. Toby took a gulp of the Scotch, wincing as the alcohol touched his cut lip. "Think he'll kill her?" he said offhandedly.

Devlin didn't answer for a long time. "I don't know," was all he finally said.

Toby shook his head and handed the bottle over the seat.

She was standing by the wall, her back to the door as she took down some Christmas garbage, and didn't turn around immediately.

"Angel Tran?" Lars said.

She finished what she was doing, before turning to look at him. "Lieutenant Morgan," she said, not surprised.

"You remember me."

"Of course. You used to give me Hershey bars when you came to see my father."

"Yes, that's right."

"And you didn't expect a quick grope in return." She crossed to the desk and sat. "But you're not here to talk about old times, right?"

"Right. I'm here to talk about the diamonds. The ones your brother tried to kill me for. My diamonds."

"That's one way to look at it, I suppose."

"That's the way I look at it. You know what's been going on here?"

"Of course."

"Of course. Your brother didn't have to die, you know. He tried to fuck with me."

"And people who fuck with Wolf get dead," she said in a tone that was vaguely mocking.

"As a rule." Lars leaned against the wall and stared down at her. "You could move into line for his share, if you cooperate."

"Big talk from a man who no longer has these diamonds."

"I intend to have them again. I will have them again. Are you interested in being on the winning side?"

"For the same ten thousand dollars you promised Phillipe? No, thank you. Not enough. I can tell you exactly when and where the stones are going to move. But for that information, I want fifty thousand dollars."

Lars smiled. "As greedy as your brother."

"But smarter, Lieutenant, much smarter."

"I can see that. As another rule of life, I never play games with smart bitches. They're too mean." He shrugged. "All right. Fifty grand."

She stared at him for a moment. "There's a phone booth by Third and Melrose. You be there in three hours. Exactly. I'll call you with the details on when and where Delvecchio's men are going to pick up the diamonds."

"Why not just tell me now?"

She smiled. "Because I'd like to be alive when you leave here."

"Fair enough."

"I'll expect payment very soon. Don't try to cheat me. Your friend at the motel can tell you that my associates are ruthless. He is only alive because we wanted it that way."

"Well, people say that I can be pretty ruthless, too, baby."

"I have heard that."

He leaned down very close to her. "It's true."

"I'll remember."

He straightened and moved toward the door. "Two questions," he said from the threshold.

"What?"

"First, why is my friend from the motel still alive?"

She smiled. "Because I wanted to deal with you. And no matter how much you want the stones, my killing him would have eliminated any chance of our working together."

"You are a smart bitch."

"The second question?"

"Why are you so willing to work with me?"

She shrugged. "Because the other side will pay me only twenty-five thousand."

"Greedy and smart." Lars shook his head and walked out.

Toby was reading the black book and didn't know that Lars had returned until the car door slammed. Without even looking back, Lars held a hand over the seat and Toby slapped the book into it. "I didn't get to the good stuff yet," he complained.

"Reardon, Tobias," Lars recited as he started the car. "Fast cock, fast mouth, and too damned nosy for his own good. Satisfied?"

Devlin gave a muffled laugh.

Lars glanced at him. "You haven't heard what it says about you, Mr. Conway."

Toby lifted the bottle for another drink. It occurred to him that they hadn't asked what happened with Angel Tran. Or even if she was still alive. But it really didn't matter. Things were getting very weird and Toby sort of wished he could just stop the world and get off. But he was also, in a strange way, enjoying himself.

He was having a good time.

46

Blue struggled to balance a large Coke, a small Tab, one foot-long hot dog (with chili, sauerkraut, onions, cheese, and relish), one plain cheeseburger, and an order of fries in the flimsy cardboard box without dumping the whole disgusting load onto his grey flannel slacks. In the front seat of a Porsche that was quite a trick.

Spaceman finally emerged from the hole-in-the-wall photography shop, a large manila envelope in one hand. "Got 'em," he announced. "Told you that bringing the film to Ivan would be a lot faster than waiting for the police lab." He slammed the car door, causing the box of food to totter dangerously.

Blue gritted his teeth and held on.

Spaceman, oblivious, shoved the envelope between his knees and started the car. "There's a little park couple blocks from here. Good place to eat."

It was a perilous trip, but the food and Blue both made it safely. Within five minutes, the two cops were sitting alone in a tiny urban excuse for a park, the lunch spread out on the grimy surface of a wooden table. Blue took one bite of the burger, then opened the envelope and dumped the contents.

What was he looking for? Evidence, maybe, whatever the hell that was. It certainly wasn't as clear in real life as in the TV cop shows. Anyway, what he saw in the first dozen or so snapshots didn't seem to prove much of anything, beyond the fact that Toby Reardon and Lars Morgan had spent a lot of time together in a cheap motel room, mostly being bored and having their picture taken. Beyond some light-hearted mugging for the camera in a few shots, they seemed pretty oblivious to the camera as they watched television, arm wrestled, shaved, and ate fast food.

"Photographic essay," Blue said. "Life on the run."

"They don't look like they're running from anybody," Spaceman said around a large bite of hot dog, chili, and kraut.

"Yeah, they certainly seemed to feel safe enough. At least, when these were taken. It must have been a real shock when the room was trashed. And somebody did a hell of a lot of bleeding. One of the them, I think, or there would have been a stiff. They might be running scared now."

"Maybe."

Abruptly, Blue stopped shuffling through the pictures. "Jesus," he said.

Spaceman looked up from the fries. "What?"

Blue fanned out several glossies. "Now we know what this is all about."

Spaceman lifted one print by the edge and studied it. "God, that ice must be worth a couple million."

"At least."

"Well, no wonder all these people have been dying." Spaceman sounded pleased. He hated mysteries, hated for things not to make sense. Now he could understand it all: The murders had happened because everybody was chasing these diamonds. Neat and clean. He picked up the chilidog again and ate with renewed enthusiasm.

Blue, however, let his cheeseburger grow cold as he went through the pile of pictures again and then a third time. He was interested in the diamonds, of course, but beyond that, he would liked to have found in the images some deeper explanation. Not for Morgan so much, but for Reardon and Conway. Was money, even so much money, enough to turn two ordinary-seeming men into ruthless killers?

Blue didn't like to think so.

Reardon had seemed intelligent and harmless enough during their interrogation. In the pictures, he was usually barefooted, shirtless, and the most obviously bored. There was one shot of him stretched out on a bed, reading the Gideon Bible and giving someone out of camera range the finger. Toby Reardon made a good gigolo, but he didn't seem like even a second-rate Dillinger.

As for Lars Morgan, though obviously a killer who struck often and easily, when viewed through Conway's expert lens he looked like anybody else. No madman. Just a slender, fair-haired man, who tossed occasional smiles at the camera, but who seemed quite unremarkable.

Blue felt very tired suddenly. He shoved all the pictures back into the envelope.

Every cop in the city was keeping an eye out for Morgan and the others. But Los Angeles was a big place, with a lot of people, and it was New Year's Eve. There was a lot going on.

Blue sat at his desk, not even looking at the pictures anymore. Instead, he was staring across the room, wondering why the hell somebody didn't take down that damned Christmas tree, which was still tilting in the corner.

He glanced at his watch. Spaceman was taking a long time at his meeting with McGannon. Or maybe he was in the can.

After another moment, Blue reached for the phone. He thought briefly, then dialed a long string of numbers. The call went through quickly, but it rang six times before a woman answered. "I know this is probably a bad time to be calling," Blue apologized. "New Year's Eve and all. But could I talk to Danny, please?"

There was a long pause.

Spaceman appeared and dropped into his chair.

The woman caught her breath finally. "Don't you know?" she said dully. "Danny's dead."

Blue thought at first that he hadn't heard her correctly. He stared at Spaceman, who was drinking an Alka-Seltzer. "What happened?" he asked at last.

"Shot himself yesterday. My husband put a gun in his mouth and pulled the trigger. I found the body. Lot of blood all over the bathroom." She told the facts wearily; it wasn't the first time. "Who is this anyway?"

Blue didn't say anything for a moment. He was aware that Spaceman was watching him curiously. "This is, ah, nobody important. I'm sorry about Danny."

"Yeah, well, maybe it was for the best. He wasn't right anymore." There was a lot of bitterness coming through her weary resignation.

"I'm sorry," he said again, then he hung up.

Spaceman folded and unfolded the empty foil packet from the Alka-Seltzer. "Something wrong?" His tone was too casual; it clearly recognized that something was very, very wrong.

Blue shoved the telephone away viciously. "Excuse me," he said in a quiet, polite voice. "I need to get some fresh air." He glared at Spaceman. "Doesn't anybody else ever notice that this place stinks?" He got up and walked out, pausing only long enough to kick the Christmas tree halfway cross the room.

Spaceman stopped at the cigarette machine before going on into the bar. Business was slow; the cops who usually came here were either on duty now or off and out for a big time someplace much grander than the old Lock-up. He had no trouble spotting Blue at a rear booth. He walked on back and slumped down across from him.

Blue had a drink, but it didn't look like he'd done much more than taste it.

Spaceman played with the new pack of cigarettes, not opening it yet. "Morell did himself in, right?"

"Right," Blue muttered.

"Too bad."

"Right," he said again.

Spaceman got tired of looking at the untouched whiskey and he picked it up for a swallow. "You're not blaming yourself, I hope."

"He was a sick man."

"True."

"Sick and hurting. Who did he come to for help? Me. God, the poor bastard made the wrong choice there, didn't he?"

"I think he was way beyond help before he ever called you. And I also think that his choice wasn't so bad."

"So why is he dead? I should have been able to do something."

"How? You just found out who the son of a bitch was. You were trying to do something."

Blue picked up the glass, stared at it, then set it down again without drinking. "I meant to call again, but we've been so damned busy."

"And we're still busy. Roy the snitch called a couple minutes ago."

"Yeah?" Blue looked interested. "What'd he have to say?"

"Street talk has it that something is coming down tonight. That's all he had."

"Tonight? Just knowing that doesn't give us anything to move on."

"True. But maybe somebody else knows more. I think we should go make some calls. Rattle a few cages." Spaceman drained the rest of the whiskey. "So much for New Year's Eve," he said glumly.

"Well, it's early yet. You might make it to Lainie's."

"Maybe. Come on, Sherlock."

Blue tossed a bill onto the table and followed Spaceman from the bar.

47

The old ice cream factory was on the eastern edge of the city, almost not in Los Angeles at all. In the early dark of December, the building was a hulking, almost frightening presence behind its chain link fence.

Maybe even Lars felt some of the threat of the place. He didn't park immediately, but instead drove around the block three times, casing the nearly empty streets. No New Year's revelers in this neighborhood.

Finally, after Devlin jumped out and pushed open the unlocked gate, Lars pulled the car into a brick cul-de-sac by the loading dock at the side of the building and turned off the engine. Suddenly it was very quiet and nobody said anything for a moment.

"Something funny, I just thought of," Devlin said finally.

"What?" Lars cracked the door open a little so that the overhead light came on. He began to check his pockets for extra clips.

"Not so long ago the most important thing in my life was whether or not the *Times* would like my damned pictures." He smiled wryly, hefting the pistol. "It's just funny, is all. I never even saw the bloody review."

Lars peered at the illuminated green dial of his watch. "I saw it," he said. "They loved the pictures. Said you were some kind of emerging genius or something like that."

"I'll be damned," Devlin muttered.

Toby, in the backseat, opened the bottle of whiskey again. "I'll drink to that," he said.

Devlin glanced at him. "I don't think you're in any shape for this thing," he said.

Toby felt like hell, but he only grunted.

Lars looked at him, then at Devlin. "This is the fucking climax. Nobody wants to miss it."

Devlin didn't say anything. He met Lars' gaze.

After a moment, Lars shrugged. "Fuck it. Tobias, remember what you were doing in 'seventy?"

"'Seventy . . . oh, yeah. My year on the point. Big thrill."

"Well, you're about to be point man again."

Toby sat up a little in the seat, ignoring the hurt in his side. "What?"

"Just so things don't get screwed up again, I want you to play forward man now."

"Which means?"

"Find a place out here where you can see just who comes in. How many. Make sure none of them are cops. That kind of thing." He reached under the seat for the Uzi. "If things go wrong, they'll go very wrong. You can make better use of this. Do something. Whatever you think will work."

Toby took the gun. "Sure, Lars," he said, "no problem." He grinned as he said it. No problem. When Lars had turned away, Toby mimicked putting the barrel of the weapon into his mouth and pulling the trigger. He realized that Devlin was watching him and grimaced.

Devlin nodded.

"So we'll see you later," Lars said, getting out of the car.

"Uh-huh," Toby said.

They were gone too quickly and Toby felt utterly alone. He sipped once more, thoughtfully, from the bottle. Well, okay. A joke: Why do old point men never die? Answer: Because they all die young. Ha, ha.

Toby closed the bottle and got out of the car, the Uzi cradled in his arm. He tried to remember if, during his wild youth, he'd ever dropped acid. He didn't think so, but this sure as hell felt like a bad-trip flashback. He moved his battered body through the darkness as lightly as he could. Black night, the feel of the gun, the taste of fear. It was all so familiar. Round and round for all these years, only to look up now and find himself right back where he'd started from.

He found a good spot: an ancient brick incinerator, the position of which would allow him a view of both the front and back entrances of the building. Perfect.

Toby settled into the dark cubby provided by the incinerator and rested the Uzi across both knees. The glow from a few unbroken street lights let him see all he needed to. More than he wanted to, in fact.

He rubbed the surface of the gun with his fingertips. Life was funny, if you stopped to think about it. Yeah, funny as hell. Who could have guessed back in Nam, playing fucking point man for crazy Lars Morgan that, all these years later, he'd be sitting on this cold brick doing the same fucking thing.

He chuckled.

It was another five minutes before something happened. That was: A van pulled up to the rear of the ice cream factory. Toby pressed himself against the grimy bricks, counting the shapes that emerged from the van. At this distance he couldn't tell who the men were, only that there were seven of them and each one was armed.

Seven, in his opinion, seemed like overkill.

While he mulled that over, two cars approached the front of the building. Five shapes got out of one and four out of the other.

Shit, this was starting to look like the fucking D-Day invasion.

Toby chewed his lower lip furiously.

Five and four and seven. Even somebody who'd flunked math could figure that out. It added up to disaster for the two men already inside the building. Not to mention the clod playing point.

Toby realized suddenly and with a knife-edged jolt of fear

that what was happening here was more than just a simple exchange of diamonds. It was an ending. Delvecchio and the Saigon bunch were tired of the whole damned charade and they were finishing it.

Toby leaned forward and closed his eyes tightly, trying to think. He wanted to throw up, the fear was so bad. He swallowed hard to get rid of the bile threatening.

Another precious minute passed before he knew what had to be done. Toby shoved the Uzi away, hiding it, and got to his feet. The only sound was that of distant traffic. No one else was in sight.

Toby took a deep breath and ran.

48

The dust on the floor tickled Devlin's nose, making him want to sneeze. He rubbed the back of one hand across his nose. How absurd. At a moment like this, all he could think of was not sneezing.

Next thing you know, he thought, I'll have to piss.

Lars scooted back and settled next to him. "Almost time," he whispered.

Devlin rubbed his nose again. "Lars," he said in a low voice, "I don't think I can kill anybody." He stared at his hands wrapped around the gun.

Lars didn't seem especially upset or even very surprised by the revelation. He just shook his head. "Well, could you at least point the damned thing at the ceiling and pull the fucking trigger? Could you do that much for me, lover?"

"Yes, sure."

"Good. Thank you very much."

Someplace, they could hear a door open and then footsteps. Devlin began to breathe through his mouth. Lars gave a deep sigh and Devlin could feel the warm, damp breath against his ear.

Spaceman tapped the dashboard impatiently. "Can't you move this thing any faster?"

Without saying anything, Blue took one hand from the

steering wheel long enough to point at the speedometer. The needle hovered at about the eighty-five MPH mark. Behind them, they could hear the sirens of several squad cars converging on the scene.

Blue returned his hand to the wheel. "Reardon didn't have an address for this place?"

"Not exactly. But I think I remember where it is. Couple years ago we busted an LSD plant there. Two of Delvecchio's men trying to go freelance. Make a left here."

The Porsche made a wheel-squealing turn. "You might give me a little more warning," Blue said with some exasperation.

Spaceman was still holding on to the dash. "What I want to know is why Reardon called us. Right here."

Blue yanked the wheel again. "He got scared," he said tightly, working to keep the car where it should be. "Toby finally got scared."

The sound of gunshots echoed from inside the factory.

Toby experienced what happened next as a series of separate moments, instants frozen in time, almost like images from Devlin's camera. It started when he kicked open the door and ran into the building. As he moved, he fired the recovered Uzi into the air.

The corridor was empty.

He ran down the hallway, toward the sound of gunshots.

Crouching in the doorway of the vast factory area, he put down a burst of covering fire. Devlin and Lars appeared, as everyone else scattered.

Lars fired at the man holding the briefcase and he fell, apparently dead.

Toby kept shooting as Lars stopped to pick up the case and then started for the door, Devlin at his side. The Uzi sent a burst of bullets over their heads. Damn, Toby thought, damn, we're going to pull this fucking thing off. Distantly, he was aware of two things suddenly: the sound of approaching sirens and the sense of someone behind him.

Before he could respond to either, a single shot rang out, very close to his ear.

Lars took one more step, started to say something, then fell.

Toby watched, stunned, as Devlin went down, too, and then picked up the fallen Walther. Scarcely seeming to aim, he fired past Toby. As the woman's body toppled over, she almost fell against Toby. He pushed her away.

"Come on," Toby yelled. "Get him up." He fired at several shadowy figures.

But Devlin didn't get up. Instead, he stayed on the ground, using his body as a shield over Lars.

Time stopped, it seemed.

Lars opened his eyes. "Put the . . . gun in my hand," he said hoarsely. "Do . . . it."

Devlin obeyed, at the same time trying uselessly to stop the blood that was gushing from Lars' chest.

"Come on, guys," Toby pleaded, scared. Someone got off a shot that hit the wall very close to his head. "Please, come on!"

Devlin picked up the briefcase and threw it at him. "Take them," he yelled. "Go!"

Toby hesitated.

As several more shots rang out, Devlin crouched lower, trying to protect Lars. Toby fired once more, then turned and got out of the building as fast as he could. No time for the car; he just kept running, clutching the briefcase to his chest.

Behind him, he could hear sirens, more shots, voices.

Blue had not been shot at since the war.

He hadn't liked it then and he didn't like it now. As they jumped from the car and headed for the door, people in dark suits seemed to be everywhere. And they all seemed to be trying to kill him.

As things turned out, it wasn't Blue who got shot.

He wanted to ask Spaceman if maybe they shouldn't wait for somebody else to do this, maybe SWAT or something, but by that time they were already inside the building, heading for the action.

A shot exploded. "Ohdamn," Spaceman said. He stumbled and fell against the wall.

Blue turned around quickly. He swore softly, then yanked a white silk handkerchief from his pocket. He dragged Spaceman out of the way. "You okay?"

"It's just a flesh wound," Spaceman said. Then he grimaced. "Flesh wounds hurt, damnit."

Some more cops ran past. Blue checked the flow of blood from Spaceman's arm; it was messy, but didn't look immediately life-threatening. "Stay here," he said, making it an order. He joined the uniforms in cleaning up the few creeps who still thought about making a fight of it.

It took only a couple more minutes to get the whole area secured. Several bodies, including that of Angel Tran, still lay where they had fallen. Blue stepped over the woman's still form and walked to where Devlin Conway sat huddled on the floor. He knelt and reached for Morgan's wrist.

"Oh, he's dead," Conway said quietly.

"You hit?"

"No." Conway smiled. "I was lucky."

Blue sighed and shook his head. He glanced back to check on Spaceman and saw the medic bent over him. That was being taken care of. Because he wanted to do this just right, he took out the Miranda card. "You're under arrest, Conway. You have the right to remain silent. If you choose to give up that right, everything you say can and will be used against you in a court of law. Do you understand?"

"Yes."

They went through the whole routine, slowly and quietly, ignoring the mayhem going on all around them.

Finally Conway said, "I probably better have a lawyer before I say anything."

"Where's Reardon?" Blue asked anyway, just for the hell of it.

"I don't know."

"How about the diamonds?"

"I don't know. And, please, no more questions until I have an attorney."

Blue nodded, pocketing the Miranda card again. "Okay."

Spaceman, still looking shaky, came over to them. "On your feet," he said to Conway. His right arm was bandaged and in a sling.

Conway nodded. He took one more look at the dead man in his lap, then carefully moved the body to the floor, and stood. Blue snapped the cuffs on him. "He'll be taken care of, right? Lars, I mean."

Spaceman snorted and walked off.

Blue put a hand on Conway's shoulder, urging him toward the door. "Don't worry about it," he said.

"Thank you."

Neither man spoke again until Conway was in the car. Blue shut the door, then leaned down to the window. "Would it do any good for me to ask you why?"

Conway leaned back against the seat and closed his eyes. There was blood all over the front of his shirt and pants, but he didn't seem aware of it. "Probably not," he said after a moment.

Blue nodded and straightened. As he did so, the glare of the police lights hit his jacket and he saw that it, too, was stained with another man's blood.

49

The bottle was empty.

Didn't matter, because there was more. And he didn't even have to get up from the table for it. Nice thing about living on a little boat like this was that everything was so convenient.

It had been a helluva job getting back here, though. Toby giggled. Three rides he managed to thumb. A Catholic priest, nice old man, but sort of befuddled, he thought Toby was an altar boy. Second car was a silver Mercedes, driven by a plump blond who invited him home for a private party. But he told her that it was against his rules to work on a holiday. The final ride, the one that delivered him almost home, was from a man Toby recognized as a former television cowboy. He was a little more diffident than the broad, but the invitation was as clear. Toby repeated his line about holidays.

Now here he was, *Homeport*, just him and a new bottle of vodka. Oh, and by the way, four million dollars worth of diamonds. His fingers trailed slowly through the stones. Maybe he should just untie the old *Homeport* and head for international waters.

But the effort involved in doing that seemed too great.

Instead, he picked up the bottle and the diamonds and went out on deck. A nice cool breeze was blowing. Across the water somebody was having a noisy party. The sound of a Lionel Richie song floated toward him. Farther away, he could hear the pop of firecrackers.

Happy New Year.

Toby picked up one of the diamonds and rubbed it thoughtfully. Pretty. Smooth. But cold. And so bloody. Too damned bloody. Without really thinking about what he was doing, Toby threw the diamond into the water. It made a small plop, a nice sound. Toby smiled a little and took a drink.

He picked up another stone and threw this one with more force. "There you go, Lars," he said. "That's for you, you crazy son of a bitch."

It was like a game. Swallow a gulp of the vodka, throw a diamond into the Pacific. The music got louder and Toby joined in on a couple of songs.

When there were just two diamonds left, Toby looked at the dock and saw those cops Kowalski and Maguire coming toward his boat. They stopped, watching him. He tossed another stone and they seemed, suddenly, to realize what he was doing. As they began to run, Toby picked up the last diamond and pitched it overboard.

50

It was very late.

Blue took a couple of glasses from the bar and filled one with brandy. The other he filled only halfway. Time to crack down on himself. What with this being the start of a New Year and all.

Spaceman was sitting on the couch, looking sleepy. Blue still wasn't sure why his partner was even here. He took the full glass and sipped gratefully. "All those diamonds," he said finally.

"All those lives," Blue reminded him, dropping onto the other end of the couch.

"You trying to be my fucking conscience?"

Blue just shook his head.

They watched dawn beginning to creep over the city. "Shouldn't you be heading out to Azusa?" Blue said. "Still time to celebrate."

"Yeah, I guess." Spaceman tugged at the sling impatiently. Blue doubted that it would last the two weeks suggested by the doctor. "I'm just not up to seeing anybody right now. Even Lainie. Not yet. You know?"

Blue did know, although he was a little surprised to hear a hard case like Kowalski actually admit it. He took a small sip of his drink, actually tasting the brandy instead of just swallowing it like medicine.

It promised to be a great twelve months ahead, if this first night was any kind of gauge. Just look at the heroic picture they made: a couple of tired, bloodied cops, watching the sun come up over their city. They cared more about the city than the city cared about them, that was for damned sure. He didn't know whether to laugh or cry.

"So happy New Year," Spaceman said finally, holding the glass aloft. "Here's to the good guys."

After a moment, Blue lifted his glass in response. "The good guys," he said.

MYSTERIOUS PRESS—

the exciting new crime imprint from Arrow Books

☐	A CAST OF KILLERS	Sidney Kirkpatrick	£2.95
☐	ROUGH CIDER	Peter Lovesey	£2.50
☐	WEXFORD: AN OMNIBUS	Ruth Rendell	£5.95
☐	WOLF TO THE SLAUGHTER	Ruth Rendell	£2.50
☐	KILL ZONE	Loren Estleman	£2.50
☐	MOONSPENDER	Jonathan Gash	£2.50
☐	HARE SITTING UP	Michael Innes	£2.50
☐	THE JUNKYARD DOG	Robert Campbell	£2.50
☐	THE COST OF SILENCE	Margaret Yorke	£2.50
☐	THE GONDOLA SCAM	Jonathan Gash	£2.50
☐	PEARLHANGER	Jonathan Gash	£2.50